The Mackinac Bride

Secrets of Mackinac Island

Katie Winters

Chapter One

1987
Mackinac Island, Michigan

Marcy Plymouth was twenty-one years old and on the brink of the rest of her life. There she stood at the edge of the Mackinac Island docks, with legs for days, slender arms, gorgeous dark blond locks, and her eyes locked expectantly on the glittering horizon of the Straits of Mackinac. In only a few minutes, the love of her life, Zane Hamlet, would appear on the steps of the Mackinac Island Shepler's Ferry. In only a few minutes, he would scoop her into his arms, kiss her with his eyes closed, and remind her, yet again, that she was meant for something more than what she'd ever known. This was the summer of her wildest dreams—June 1987, and it was only just beginning.

"Hey there, Marcy!" Kurt, one of the head ferry operators at Shepler's, stepped from the mainland onto the dock and waved. As Marcy and Kurt were both islanders through-and-through, they'd known one another since they'd been diaper-wearing toddlers and thought of one another as family.

"There he is." Marcy extended her arms, wrapping Kurt in a playful hug, then bounced back. "That uniform is really something on you."

Kurt guffawed, the tops of his cheeks turning bright red with embarrassment. "I thought I looked important in it. Nothing like Marcy Plymouth to knock me down a peg."

"Don't sell yourself short," Marcy scolded him. "You look like a captain."

"Yeah, yeah. Tease me all you like."

"I'm serious, Kurt. You've worked hard to get where you are. It's rare to be named captain at twenty-one. You should be proud."

Kurt's blue eyes pierced hers as he palmed the back of his neck. "I guess you're waiting for Zane?"

It was Marcy's turn to blush. Her face burned hot with excitement. "I probably look so foolish, waiting here at the dock for him like a golden retriever. But I just can't wait!" Marcy then extended her hand out to allow the engagement ring on her fourth finger to glint in the penetrating June sunlight. "I just can't believe that I'll be Mrs. Hamlet before the end of the summer."

"It's the wedding of the season," Kurt quipped.

"And you've already got a date lined up for yourself? I told you that you have a plus one," Marcy reminded him.

"I've got a few options in mind."

"Kurt!" Marcy whacked him playfully on the upper arm. "You have to stop running girls around."

Kurt gestured toward his captain's uniform and wagged his eyebrows. "Babe, haven't you seen the uniform? I can do what-ever I want."

Marcy rolled her eyes deep into the back of her head, even

as a smile played out across her lips. "You'll never settle down, will you?"

"Why would I? I've got my eyes set on a lifetime of adventure," Kurt continued. "This captain job is only the beginning. I have a hunch that it'll land me somewhere exciting. Somewhere like the Florida Keys or Hawaii."

"Somewhere far, far away," Marcy offered, jutting out her lower lip.

"Don't pretend like Zane isn't going to whisk you away," Kurt said. "The man's an architect now. He's probably got his sights on a thousand jobs across the country. For all I know, you'll be in Paris or Rome by the end of the summer."

Marcy's heart performed a backflip. Was it really possible that her life would take on such dimension? All she'd ever known was Mackinac Island, plus a smattering of other Northern Michigan cities, towns, lakes, and fields. Her father, Elliott Plymouth, had owned the Pink Pony Bar and Grill for as long as anyone could remember. Since the age of fourteen, Marcy had worked there as well, often for less pay than the other workers. The job was required of her as a Plymouth. That was just the way things were. "It is what it is" was an expression her father liked to say. Marcy resented this expression, although she understood why Elliott used it so often. His life had not been an easy one.

Perhaps Marcy's would become easy soon. Or, better yet, perhaps her life would glow with magic.

"There's the boat!" Kurt pointed out across the water, then adjusted his captain's hat on his head and explained that he would be driving the boat back across the Straits in fifteen minutes. Already, tourists lined up along the dock, shifting against their suitcases and touching their sunburns tentatively.

Marcy could hardly understand anything Kurt said. The moment the ferry docked and dropped its ramp, her heart burst into her throat, and her ears ceased to hear. All she could do was feel— feel the love that beamed from Zane's eyes and the hope that brewed between them.

Zane was handsome and had always been handsome, which, Marcy liked to say, was "besides the point." Yes, he was six foot three, with broad shoulders, thick black hair, and glittering, inky eyes. But beyond that, he was quick-witted, incredibly kind, and intelligent without being boastful. Above all that, of course, he loved her with a passion and a fire that Marcy knew was unparalleled. Her female friends on the island were terribly jealous of her stories. All she could do was thank her lucky stars.

Zane stepped off the boat and did precisely what Marcy had expected him to do. He took her into his arms, kissed her with his eyes closed, and whispered, "This will be the best summer of our lives." Marcy fell into him like she fell into daydreams. It was hardly possible that he was real.

Zane and Marcy collected Zane's two suitcases and headed up the dock, piercing through the throng of tourists to get to the main road. Once there, Marcy remembered to turn back to wave to Kurt, who waved from the top of the boat.

"Kurt looks good in the captain uniform," Zane said with a hearty laugh.

"I think so, too. Each time I compliment him about it, he thinks I'm teasing him," Marcy offered, turning her head to gaze into Zane's eyes.

"The man's just in love with you. That's all," Zane returned.

"That's just stupid," Marcy returned. "Everyone on this island knows that I gave my heart to you five summers ago."

"Five? I thought it was six," Zane quipped.

Marcy stuck out her tongue. "You were all wrapped up with Zoey Carlson six summers ago."

"Oh, I was not. I had my heart set on you. I just flirted with Zoey to make you jealous."

Marcy shivered with giggles and again fell into him, closing her eyes as they kissed. Several months ago, when he'd visited during a heinous springtime storm, they'd burrowed up in his parents' vacation house, eaten snacks, drunk wine, and conspired about their future. It was over that weekend that he'd asked her to marry him, showing her the ring he'd selected at a vintage shop in East Lansing, Michigan. The *"yes"* had spilled out of her without question. *"I love you, Zane Hamlet. I've wanted to marry you every single day since I met you."*

As Zane and Marcy turned the corner onto Main Street, Marcy's heart dropped into her belly. Along the side of the Pink Pony, at least twenty people either waited or sipped drinks, their faces pinched with annoyance at the wait time.

"Wow. The bar's getting good business these days," Zane commented.

"Maybe we should go back to your place another way," Marcy stuttered softly, suddenly frightened. "I told my dad specifically that I needed this day off."

"And you never take a day off," Zane reminded her.

"Exactly. He hardly hires new staff because he just relies on me to pick up the slack," Marcy blurted, then scrunched her nose as she added, "I know that sounds crass. It's our family business. I have to be there for him. For us."

"But what's he going to do when we get out of here?" Zane asked softly, his eyes captivating her with their magic.

Marcy's own eyes welled with tears. "He'll have to figure something out."

"And he will because that's what people do. They figure something out. They survive."

At that moment, Elliott Plymouth's voice boomed out across Main Street. He'd pummelled out of the front door of the Pink Pony, turned his head, and spotted his one and only daughter. "Marcy? If you walk away from this mess, you can forget about receiving your paycheck this week."

Marcy's stomach flipped over. Zane cupped her hand tenderly and lifted his chin in greeting. He stepped forward, guiding Marcy toward the bouncing chaos of the Pink Pony.

"Good afternoon, Mr. Plymouth," Zane said, sounding more like a businessman than anything. "I think Marcy told you that it's my first day on the island after over a month. I just graduated from Michigan State, and Marcy and I have plans to celebrate."

This, too, turned Marcy's stomach. She'd wanted to get time off to visit Zane in East Lansing for his graduation, but her father had refused. *"He'll be up here in no time. And besides, what's a graduation? It's just a bunch of pomp and circumstance and people wearing silly hats. I need you at the bar."*

"I'm sure you two can find time to celebrate tomorrow," Elliott barked. "Marcy, I've got a line-up of ten people waiting for their beers. Greg is messing with a busted keg, and I can't get a hold of that new girl, Stacy."

Marcy knew that Stacy had quit without bothering to tell anyone. A recent incident with Elliott had been enough to drive Stacy off the island and back to her small town in Illinois. *"Your dad is the worst,"* Stacy had said.

Marcy felt wordless and helpless. Her father's eyes were rimmed with red, and his voice was edged with panic. Just a glance at the Pink Pony told her that everyone involved was in over their heads. This was her family's bar; this was her blood.

On top of it all, very soon, she would abandon this bar for greener pastures with Zane. Maybe if she gave her father a little more time at the bar, he would "bless" her decision to leave. Not that she'd gotten around to telling him that she and Zane planned to leave.

"Just let me get them through this rush," Marcy blurted to Zane, whose shoulders dropped with sorrow. She squeezed his bicep and winced. "I'm sorry. But you know how it is on the

6

BUSINESS REPLY MAIL

FIRST-CLASS MAIL   PERMIT NO. 107   BOONE IA

POSTAGE WILL BE PAID BY ADDRESSEE

NYRJ3BS3A

THE
NEW YORKER

PO BOX 37617
BOONE, IA 50037-2617

NO POSTAGE
NECESSARY
IF MAILED
IN THE
UNITED STATES

THE
NEW YORKER

Subscribe and save up to 60% off the cover price.

Plus get a free notebook with your paid subscription.

Offer valid in the U.S. only. First issue mails within 3 weeks. Please add applicable sales tax. *The New Yorker* publishes weekly, except for four planned combined issues, as indicated on the issue's cover, and other combined or extra issues.

☐ 26 weeks for just $3.50 a week
   ($91 total)

☐ 52 weeks for just $3.25 a week
   ($169 total)

By subscribing, you agree to our user agreement (condenast.com/user-agreement) and privacy policy and cookie statement including your California rights (condenast.com/privacy-policy).

Name _____ PLEASE PRINT _____

Address _____ Apt. _____

City _____ State _____ Zip _____

E-mail _____

Order online and SAVE UP TO $10.
Go to newyorker.com/go/savenow2A

☐ Payment enclosed

island during tourist season. This is the only time we make real money."

Zane sniffed, then eyed Elliott. "I'm tired after the drive, anyway." He said it like he didn't really mean it. "Why don't you come up to the house after you get off? Mr. Plymouth, you promise you won't keep her past nine?"

"You don't have any say in her schedule until you say, 'I do,'" Elliott replied coolly.

Marcy's heart shattered at the clear arrogance in her father's words. Oh, how she loved him! How she ached for the pain and the darkness in his heart!

"It's okay," Marcy pleaded with Zane not to push the matter. "I'll bring pizza on the way up to your place. We'll stay up all night if we have to."

Zane's eyes were fierce. He glanced at Elliott, then back at Marcy, before he dropped a kiss on her cheek, took the other suitcase from her hand, and said, "Always a pleasure to see you, Mr. Plymouth." He then walked past him and began his long trek up to the vacation house his family had owned for generations.

Marcy watched him go, telling herself that he understood her predicament. After all, she and Zane were linked forevermore. There was nothing that they couldn't understand or get through together. Yes, Elliott Plymouth was problematic. But very soon, he would be just a part of their past as they built a fresh future together. She couldn't wait.

Chapter Two

Present Day

E lise Darby sat in the second row of business class on the flight from LA to Detroit. There in the cushioned seat (that could extend all the way back into a bed), she enjoyed a glass of sparkling champagne, a platter of fine cheeses and Italian salami, an additional glass of champagne, and an entire movie that had only been released a couple of months before. Exhausted after two weeks hard at work in Los Angeles, she allowed herself the full luxuries of the flight— cozying up in the blanket they'd given her and cracking jokes with the flight attendant who cared for her every need. In just a few weeks, Elise Darby would walk down the aisle as a bride; after all her hard work on the film, it was time to start celebrating.

"A screenwriter? How exciting," the flight attendant chatted as she searched through the plane's dessert options and placed a tiramisu on the extended table. "But what brings you to Michigan?"

"I moved there," Elise replied with a romantic, slightly tipsy sigh. "I have family on Mackinac Island, and while visiting them there, I fell in love."

"Oh, how romantic!" The flight attendant tilted her head adoringly and looked on the verge of swooning. "Tell me everything about him."

"Excuse me? Miss?" A woman two rows back demanded the flight attendant's attention, which she clearly did not want to give. The flight attendant wrinkled her nose and gave Elise a knowing look, as though the two of them were in cahoots. "Hold that thought."

Elise laughed as she dug her fork into the soft cream of the tiramisu. All summer long and into September, she'd kept up a semi-strict "bride diet" to slip easily into the dress that her half-sister, the ever-fashionable Tracey, had picked out for her. Then again, Elise's mother had always taught her that travel days weren't diet days. "It's better to enjoy your life than whittle yourself away," Allison Darby had said, her eyes twinkling.

Elise's mother, Allison, had died a little more than a year ago. Although Elise had lived at least ten lifetimes since then, her world still felt emptier and less sunny. Allison had been Elise's very best friend and confidant. Now, Elise felt like she lived life without a script, so to speak. Allison was no longer there to guide her or give her advice. All she had left were her memories.

The plane landed in Detroit at seven-thirty that evening. Elise thanked the flight attendant for her extra assistance during the flight, tipping her as she stepped toward the front of the plane. The flight attendant brimmed with happiness, adding, "You tell that handsome man of yours that he's the luckiest in the world."

Once off the plane, Elise grabbed a cup of coffee, waited for her suitcases, and then headed to the long-term parking lot to pick up her vehicle. Once there, she loaded her suitcases in the back and sat in the driver's seat for the better part of five minutes, exhausted after such a long flight, yet overwhelmed with pleasure at everything that had happened so far that month. It was the end of September, and Michigan had rushed full-speed-ahead toward autumn, lining the tree leaves with red, orange, and yellow and adding a welcome crisp to the air. Out in the Midwest, away from the heat and smog of Los Angeles, Elise could breathe properly. She couldn't wait to return to the island.

The drive from Detroit to Mackinac wasn't an easy one. Elise decided to grab a hotel room for the night, sleep as long as she pleased, and then take her sweet time up to Mackinac the following day. By the time she reached the Mackinaw City docks to board Shepler's Ferry, it was five-thirty in the afternoon, only thirty minutes before Wayne's shift at The Grind Coffee House was due to be finished. Since she'd learned his schedule, it had been her plan to surprise him.

The ride across the Straits to Mackinac Island took approximately sixteen minutes. Although Elise was accustomed to the ferry by now, she still loved to stand in the sweet chill of the top deck and watch the red, orange, and yellow trees of the island swell toward her. As a writer, she was endlessly nostalgic and loved to dive deep into her first memories of Mackinac Island, when she'd arrived as a stranger, was nearly chased off the island by her half-brother, Alex, and eventually found a brand-new family of her own. The story was a whirlwind, one that would be coming to cinemas everywhere the following year. Elise had once joked that the film should be called "My messy, messy life."

Kurt, the ferry boat captain, stepped out from the captain's office to greet Elise warmly. He was broad-shouldered and muscular in his captain's uniform, which he'd told Elise was "a second skin" at that point. Apparently, he'd worked as a Shepler's captain since the year 1987. When he didn't work on the ferry, he helped out at the Pink Pony alongside Marcy. Elise was pretty sure the two were approximately the same age. When together, they seemed thick as thieves, with a sort of separate "language" that they used when they spoke to each other. One could say just a couple of words that made no sense to anyone else, and the other would burst into laughter. Their friendship was for the ages.

Once, Elise had asked Cindy whether or not Kurt and Marcy had ever been a couple. To this, Cindy had shaken her head wildly. *"Marcy just isn't a romantic person,"* she'd explained. This had bothered Elise. *Who wasn't a romantic person?* She couldn't comprehend that.

"How are you doing, Kurt?" Elise asked.

"Not bad. Not bad." Kurt's smile widened, showing the tops of his sun-tanned cheeks, which he'd earned after many summers on the top decks of Shepler's ferries. "Just another few weeks of working the ferries, and then I'll settle into another Mackinac winter."

"I guess Marcy will steal you for some shifts at the Pink Pony?" Elise asked.

Kurt's eyes twinkled knowingly. "She hates to admit that she sometimes needs my help up there. You know how Marcy is. She doesn't like to ask for help."

Elise's laughter echoed out across the Straits.

"I heard that that nephew of yours had a baby!" Kurt said, tilting his head.

"Oh, yes." Elise's heart lifted, remembering Michael, Cindy's son. "Michael, Margot, and Winnie are all very happy and healthy. I've been out in Los Angeles for two weeks, so I haven't gotten as much baby time as I would have liked. Cindy's been sending me some pretty cute pictures, though." Elise turned her phone to show the images of Cindy acting the part of a brand-new grandmother by taking an endless array of photos from numerous angles. As far as new grandmothers were concerned, there were never enough photos.

"Adorable," Kurt said with a sigh. "Michael was always such a ruffian. Hard to believe that he settled down."

Elise giggled. "Now it's your turn."

"No way, José," Kurt joked. "This bachelor can't be tamed."

Elise's heart was shadowed by the thought. *Was Kurt actually happy as a bachelor? Had he ever wanted to be a father or a husband? Or was he content to work at the Pink Pony and Shepler's Ferry, even into his fifties?*

It wasn't up to Elise to judge. All sorts of people lived all sorts of ways.

Once at the ferry docks on Mackinac Island, Elise waved goodbye to Kurt, grabbed the handles of her suitcases, and tugged them down the small cobblestone path that led to The Grind. Although tourist season flickered to a close, a smattering of tourists remained outside, sipping lattes and showing each other pictures from their vacations. Inside, Wayne was bent over the counter, probably doing inventory. Michael's shadow lurked in the back. Since they'd begun working at The Grind as partners, Wayne and Michael had created a lovely balance, one that allowed them plenty of days off plus a good salary and health insurance for Michael. As a new father, this was essential.

It warmed Elise's heart that Wayne had created stability in his nephew's life, especially because Michael had been, in Kurt's words, "a ruffian." He'd disappeared for the better part of three years without telling anyone where he'd been. Cindy had been a nervous wreck.

Elise appeared at the counter of The Grind and watched as Wayne whispered to himself as he took notes.

"I'll be right with you," he told Elise, who he probably thought was just another customer.

"No rush!" Elise chimed back.

At this, Wayne's chin jumped up. His eyes glittered with love and recognition. With a flash, he leaped around the counter, grabbed Elise around the waist, lifted her onto the counter, and dove forward to kiss her. It was the stuff you read about in romance novels; it was better than any romantic comedy Elise had ever seen. With her heart in her throat, Elise allowed herself to break their kiss, if only to whisper, "I missed you so much." Her heart burst with love for him.

"You don't even know," Wayne returned, dotting his nose upon hers.

"What's gotten into you two? You know, you're not teenagers anymore." Michael appeared in the doorway, grinning wildly from behind a large box that he held aloft.

"Hi, Mike." Elise rolled her eyes and dropped off the counter. "How's that darling baby of yours?"

"She's a crier," Michael replied with a laugh. "I told her that she can use that voice of hers as much as she wants. She's opinionated, to say the least."

Elise and Wayne laughed appreciatively.

"You must be tired," Elise said.

Michael shrugged. "I know it sounds cheesy, but it's worth it."

"I know," Elise breathed, remembering when she'd held her babies in her arms, so sleep-deprived that she couldn't see straight. She'd been grateful for every single moment with them. Sometimes, she ached to have those moments back. "Enjoy it."

"I will," Michael promised.

When Michael disappeared into the back, Wayne palmed the back of his neck and said, "Let's get out of here. Let's celebrate! You're back!"

"Wedding in T-Minus twenty-six days!" Elise shrieked as her eyes widened.

Wayne pumped his fist into the air, then gathered his things and said goodbye to Michael. "We're out for the night. See you later?"

Elise left her suitcases at The Grind for the evening, then headed out into the evening for a drink. Of course, the only bar in the area that suited them was The Pink Pony. It drew them like a powerful magnet. As Wayne pressed open the door, his eyes flashed back toward Elise's as he breathed, "Please, don't be mad."

"About what?" Elise asked.

But in a flash, she understood. As they entered, the entire Swartz family burst from the side table, calling out, "Welcome home!" and rushing toward her, their arms stretched out. Immediately, Elise was pressed into Cindy, then Tracey, then Emma, then Alex, and then Dean. The table was heavy with pizza, French fries, onion rings, and even a few salads (a rarity this late in the season in the Midwest).

"You've got to be kidding me," Elise blurted, her eyes flashing back toward Wayne's.

Wayne shrugged. "Your sisters talked me into it."

Elise's mouth parted with surprise as she glared playfully at both Cindy and Tracey, who shrugged. "We convinced Penny to tell us exactly when you'd be back," Cindy explained.

"That girl! She's always up to no good," Elise quipped.

"How did the last few shoots go?" Tracey asked, her eyes alight.

"Oh, it was fantastic," Elise explained as she sat across from her, crossing her ankles beneath her. "Malcolm really brought his A-game the past few weeks. I adored working with him."

Tracey's eyes twinkled knowingly. When the film had shot out on Mackinac Island, Tracey had been one of the hardest workers in the costume department, where she'd met and become very (very) friendly with the director of the film, Malcolm. Although their relationship had certainly been romantic, Malcolm had a young, deaf daughter out in Los Angeles and couldn't possibly leave his life there for Tracey. On top of it all, Tracey's daughter, Emma, was now pregnant with her first child. As the father wasn't in the picture, it was up to Tracey to support Emma and her new grand baby.

It was just a matter of bad timing, Elise knew. But it still cracked her heart in two.

"You look sun-tanned and happy," Dean said from the other side of Alex, who smiled good-naturedly. "You should have brought a bit of that sun back with you. We've had a chilly last few weeks of September."

"But we usually have gorgeous, blue-skied Octobers," Cindy assured Elise knowingly. "I don't know why more people don't have weddings here on the island in the autumn. October 22.nd is bound to be a banner day."

Under the table, Wayne squeezed Elise's hand. Elise's heart surged into her throat. After several weeks of non-stop meetings, film shoots, work emails, and work phone calls, it was miraculous to be surrounded by so much love.

"Hi, honey." Marcy Plymouth appeared at the end of the table, her hands on her slender hips. At fifty-six, she was gorgeous, with fantastic skin that she'd clearly taken good care of, a runner's build, and a dye job that maintained her dark blond hair. "Glad to see you've made it back from California."

"Marcy! It's good to be back."

Since Elise's initial interactions with Marcy, she'd adored her. Marcy was part of the heart and soul of Mackinac, an ever-present face during Elise's first very lonely weeks. It wasn't always clear to Elise whether or not Marcy liked her back just as much, as Marcy kept to herself and didn't reveal much about her heart or her mind.

Marcy took Elise and Wayne's drink orders and soon

returned with white wine for Elise and a beer for Wayne. Elise lifted her wine and said, "I don't mean to put pressure on you, Marcy, but I couldn't help but notice that you haven't yet RSVP'd to our wedding."

Marcy cocked her eyebrow. Was she annoyed that Elise had put her on the spot like this?

"It just wouldn't feel right without you there," Elise added hurriedly. "You've been a part of my Mackinac life since I got here."

Marcy nodded ever-so-slightly and shifted her weight. "I'll have to really think about it, Elise."

"Marcy is anti-romance," Cindy teased, flashing Elise a smile. "She's a cynical bartender, through and through."

"It's the only way to do this kind of job," Marcy tried to joke. "The things I've seen working at this very bar would tear you apart."

"What kinds of things?" Elise asked, eager to hear Marcy's jokes.

"Let's just put it this way," Marcy said, her eyes sparkling. "What I've seen in this bar makes it clear to me that men are just about the most useless things there are." She then flashed a smile to Wayne, Alex, and Dean and added, "Except for you three, of course."

"No offense taken, Marcy," Wayne returned with a boisterous laugh.

"I'll get you started on another drink, Alex?" Marcy asked, switching to her "business" voice.

Something in Marcy's mannerisms made Elise think that Marcy was somehow anxious about the topic of romance. *But why?*

As Marcy rushed back behind the bar to grab Alex's next beer, Dean asked her another question about Los Angeles and about her son, Brad, who remained out there. Elise's thoughts about Marcy faded as she allowed herself to fall into the swell of her family's love. Conversation and laughter spilled through the night. Only later, as she began to fall into a hazy sleep back at the house she now shared with Wayne, did she remember the strange glimmer in Marcy's eyes— proof, maybe, that romance was a source of pain for her. *But what had happened? And why didn't she give herself a chance to try again?*

Chapter Three

Thursday morning, Marcy returned from her five a.m. six-mile run, scrubbed herself clean in the apartment she now lived in alone above the Pink Pony (the very one she'd been raised in), dried her hair, added just a smidge of makeup, bundled up, and then headed out into the crisp chill. It was September 29th, the very start of autumn, but clouds already seemed like a permanent ceiling above Mackinac— a reminder of the encroaching darkness of the winter. It would be another winter alone.

Marcy was pleased to see that Kurt was the captain that morning on the Shepler's Ferry. Just as ever, he wore that captain's uniform and his captain's hat and sauntered across the deck with the confidence of a much-younger man. He'd poured her a mug of coffee from the little coffee maker he had on board, and together, they leaned against the railing on the boat and watched as the last straggling tourists entered the ferry below. *How many times had they ridden this same ferry together, forward and back? It had to have been in the millions at this point.*

"Can I count on you for a couple of shifts this weekend?" Marcy asked, nearly scalding her tongue with the coffee.

"Sure thing," Kurt replied. "Pink Pony is about the best place in the world during these autumn and winter months. The only source of drama, anyway."

"You love the drama at the Pink Pony," Marcy said, grinning sheepishly. "Sometimes I think you might start it yourself, just for something to talk about."

"You're a cynic, Marcy Plymouth," Kurt rhymed playfully.

Marcy retreated downstairs with her coffee to sit at the window and watch the rushing waves. Up top, Kurt greeted the ferry travelers via microphone and thanked them for choosing Shepler's Mackinac Island Ferry. In the corner of the seating area, a little baby blinked his blue eyes toward Marcy expectantly, as though he'd known her all his young life. Marcy turned her eyes away immediately, always too frightened of the feelings of regret that swelled within her when she interacted with babies for too long.

She hadn't been allowed to live that life. It was better not to think about it.

Once at the Mackinaw City ferry docks, Marcy bid goodbye to Kurt and said, "See you in a few hours." She then stepped off the ferry, adjusted her backpack, and headed out for the fifteen-minute walk to the nearby garage where she kept the beat-up car she drove when she was off the island. She paid a small monthly rate to keep it there, which was all the more essential given the recent circumstances. Like it or not, she needed a car these days.

Once on the road, Marcy toyed around with the radio station before she discovered "all the hits of the eighties," which had been "her golden era." Olivia Newton-John howled through "Let's Get Physical" right before Daryl Hall and John Oates sang "Sara Smile." Marcy's heart swelled with a mix of sorrow and nostalgia as images raced through her mind. "Get a grip, Marcy," she told herself at a stoplight. A split-second later, the radio hits stopped for a commercial break. Marcy breathed a sigh of relief.

Marcy reached the Cheboygen Retirement Home at eleven-thirty that morning. Just like always, she parked in the very last row of the parking lot, still grateful for her sporty body and all it could do.

Once inside the retirement facility, Marcy greeted Nellie, the young woman at the front desk. "Hi there, Nellie."

"Oh, hello, Marcy." Nellie smiled serenely. Marcy almost always wondered why a young woman like Nellie wanted to work in a place like this. *Didn't she have dreams?*

"I'm here to see the old man," Marcy quipped, trying to joke.

Nellie chuckled. "I'm sure he'll be happy to see you. You can head on back."

Marcy walked slowly through the hallways of the retirement facility, which always smelled vaguely like hospital food and cleaning supplies. Still, it was the best facility in the area, especially for what the doctors described as her father's "unspecified memory condition." What Elliott Plymouth suffered from wasn't exactly "Alzheimer's," per se. But the anger, the lack of comprehension, and the lack of short-term memory had made him very difficult to care for during his final few months at home. The facility had seemed the only way to keep Marcy from going insane herself.

The move had happened about two and a half years ago, at this point, with much of the Pink Pony revenue going straight to the medical facility and any and all "experimental" memory drugs. These days, Elliott Plymouth was in his early eighties—an age that anyone should be grateful to reach, Marcy knew. Her mother had certainly never reached that age. Plenty of people hadn't.

Then again, Elliott Plymouth was one of the only people who Marcy loved in the entire world. His memory slipping away tore her up inside far more than she'd imagined it would. That was the thing about grief. You never knew how it would get you.

"Hi, Dad." Marcy stepped into the shadows of Elliott's suite to find Elliott in his armchair, his face glowing with the light of the television. He was watching a game show, one where people had to guess the cost of ordinary items.

Elliott looked disgruntled. He glanced her way, casting her a surly glance, but then immediately repaired it as he realized who she was. "Oh. Hi, honey." He tried on a smile that immediately fell from his face.

Marcy perched at the edge of his couch and smiled, trying to pretend she was as young and happy as Nellie, the woman at the front desk. "How are you doing today?"

Elliott pointed toward the television. "They're playing the same TV episode that they played last week."

Marcy cocked her head. *Was that true?* If so, that meant that Elliott's short-term memory wasn't as bad as the doctors had said. Then again, maybe it was a fluke.

"They shouldn't get away with that," Marcy affirmed.

"You're telling me. I pay all this money for cable, and this is the crap they pull?" Elliott said, trying on the arrogant tone that Marcy remembered so well from her youth.

Marcy was half-grateful for this, half-annoyed. Her father had never been particularly easy to be around. Then again, when he brought that "tone" out, he seemed more like his old self. How could she miss the man who'd once made her life a living hell? She just did.

After a bit of small talk that didn't really go anywhere, Marcy ordered lunch from the downstairs cafeteria and waited with her father for their order to arrive. When it did, she set up their turkey burgers, sweet potato fries, and salad on a little table and insisted they sit together. In turn, Elliott insisted that they eat with the television on. Marcy had fought and lost that battle enough times to know not to push it. The TV would remain.

Once at the table, Elliott took a small bite of his turkey burger and complained that it wasn't "real meat." Marcy reminded him that this was healthier for him as she played around with the lettuce in her salad.

"The bar's been going really well," she decided to tell him, unsure of what else to talk about. "We were just written up in 'top places to eat and drink' in *Michigan Monthly*. I swear, I always have a line around the block during busy summer nights."

Elliott made a strange noise in his throat. Marcy wasn't sure if he'd actually heard her. He took another bite of his burger, grimaced, and turned his head to watch the television again. Not for the first time that week, Marcy asked herself why she bothered to drive to Cheboygen about twelve times per month. *Was it guilt? Or fear of what would happen if she left him alone?*

"I'm going to need your help all summer long," Elliott grumbled then, his tone just the same as it ever was. "You have to cut ties with that Zane character. What he's after and what you're after are two different things. You remember where you came from. You're an islander, girl. You hear?"

Marcy's jaw dropped with surprise. In all the years since that final summer, Marcy hadn't heard her father say Zane's name once. A shiver rushed up and down her spine. Hunger was now the furthest thing from her mind.

On television, some guy from Illinois made a wild guess for a can of tuna, one that seemed totally inaccurate. Elliott then began to berate the man on television, telling him that he didn't deserve his slot on the show. Marcy took the opportunity to put her burger down, step into the bathroom, close the door, and weep into her hands.

It was now 2022— thirty-five years after the "best summer of her life." A rogue comment from her father about Zane shouldn't have broken her up inside. But it had. Oh, it had.

Chapter Four

Saturday afternoon brought surprising weather in the upper sixties. Marcy stood in front of the Pink Pony with her hands propped up on her lower back, and her cheeks lifted toward the sun. In only a few minutes, she would open her door to the throng of weekend tourists, all of whom wished to grab and hold onto the last dregs of summertime. They'd need beers, rum runners, and glasses of wine to prove their merriment. They'd need Marcy.

"Excuse me? Are you open?" Three women in their early thirties hustled down the cobblestones, giggling. The one in the center wore a "Bride to Be" banner across her chest. Just as ever, Marcy's gut swirled with panic and nostalgia at the sight of a bride-to-be. If only she could bottle the spirit of a bride. If only she could fully remember what that time had been like.

"Just about," Marcy replied, flashing the women a knowing smile. "Why don't you grab a table out here in the sun? I'll get you some menus."

Once inside the Pink Pony, Marcy arranged the sliced lemons and limes behind the bar counter and watched the three women sit in the glittering autumn sun. Jealousy burned through her. Just as she stacked the food and drink menus in her arms, a text message buzzed through her cell. It was Kurt.

KURT: Hey! I'll head over to the PP in about five minutes. Need me to grab anything?

The majority of the Pink Pony staff members had high-tailed it for their "real lives" in other states, other capitols, and other warmer climates. This left Marcy in a lurch, so to speak, for the autumn and winter months. She was grateful that Kurt had agreed, yet again, to step in and pick up the slack. As they'd been friends for what felt like eons at that point, they often worked seamlessly, reading one another's minds during the particularly hazy nights when each table and bar stool was filled with a very thirsty customer.

Marcy hurriedly texted him back.

MARCY: I think I'm good on supplies. Just need a quick set of hands. :)

MARCY: I can already feel how ravenous the tourists are today. It's the last of the beautiful autumn days. They'll run us dry.

Marcy suited up the bride-to-be and her friends with glasses of champagne and a cheese platter, then rushed back into the Pink Pony to wait on two guys who asked that football be played on one of the television screens.

"State plays at two," one of them told her simply, as though Michigan State's football schedule was like church, a necessity.

"Yeah, yeah. I know." Marcy teased him and flicked through the channels to find the football game. "I take it you boys want a round of beers? Can I interest you in some wings? Fries? Onion rings?"

The men nodded gleefully, ready to dive into an afternoon of gluttony and sports. Just as another three tables' worth of people arrived, Kurt rushed through the door, adjusting his baseball hat. Instead of his traditional captain's uniform, he'd donned a pair of worn jeans and a blue button-down t-shirt. Fifty-six, Kurt had taken rather good care of himself over the years, with just the slightest of paunches that hung above his belt buckle. He greeted Marcy playfully, dropped his jacket behind the counter, and then immediately hustled over to find a table for the newest guests. Marcy's heart swelled with appreciation.

The truth of it was that since Marcy had arrived back from the nursing home a few days back, she hadn't been able to get out of her bad mood. Her father hadn't mentioned the name "Zane" in what felt like eons. Now, Marcy's heart screamed the name at every turn, as though it wanted to put Marcy through the same misery that she'd escaped thirty-five years ago.

It wasn't that Marcy wanted to feel sorry for herself. On Mackinac Island especially, however, she was constantly a witness to romances, beautiful family parties, engagements, bridal parties, and other celebrations that allowed people to walk the "appropriate" path of life. Why hadn't she been allowed to walk that path? Had she done something wrong?

During a very brief lull in Pink Pony traffic later that afternoon, Kurt trounced behind the bar in that playful and joyful way of his, grabbed a pickle from the pickle jar, took a bite, and said, "How's it hanging, Marcy? I haven't heard a peep from you in a few days."

Marcy lifted a shoulder, not in any mood to joke around. "Just fine."

Kurt stuttered slightly, fully recognizing that she was a bit sour. He lowered his voice knowingly. "What's going on? Did something happen in Cheboygen?"

Kurt was just about the only person who knew anything about Marcy's current life. When Marcy had first come up with the idea of getting a suite for her father at the Cheboygen retirement facility, Kurt had urged her to do it. "You've been miserable for years. You can't expect yourself to go through this, day after day and night after night, for the rest of his life."

Initially, Marcy had fought back, saying that Marcy was the only person Elliott had. Very soon after, when Elliott had thrown a hot skillet across the kitchen they'd shared for over fifty years, Marcy finally made the call. Kurt had been right, no matter how little she'd wanted to admit it. Maybe he was the only person in the world who had her best interests at heart.

But that didn't mean that Marcy wanted to tell him about what her father had said back in Cheboygen. Zane was a no-go zone. Marcy had made that clear thirty-five years ago.

Finally, Marcy found her voice. "Naw. Dad's fine. I'm just a bit quiet today, is all."

Marcy then used the excuse that the bride out front needed a refill of champagne and fled out the door and into the glittering sun. Outside, a horse and buggy clopped past, upon which a young, newly married couple sat, locked in an embrace as they watched the world go by outside. The bride-to-be and her friends waved at the happy couple, practically swooning.

"Can I get you another drink?" Marcy asked the bride-to-be.

"Oh, yes. Oh, please." The bride-to-be looked overwhelmed. "And perhaps another cheese plate? Or is that crazy, girls?"

Her friends admitted that they could "always eat more." Marcy returned to the kitchen, where she asked the two chefs on-hand if they could prepare a cheese plate. She then popped a bottle of champagne and returned to the table, where only the two friends of the bride remained.

"We just can't thank you enough for making today so special for us," one of the bride's friends said to Marcy, her voice syrupy and overly sweet.

"Yes. Brittany has had a very hard go of it," the other woman said, furrowing her brow.

Marcy shifted her hip, slightly intrigued. It always seemed that after a certain point at night, people who drank at The Pink Pony made it their mission to tell Marcy every single secret in their souls. As it was still only five-fifteen, it was a rather early time for such secret divulgence. *But whatever. Bring it on.*

"Yeah. She was engaged when we were in our twenties," the first friend said under her breath, watching the door to ensure that the bride didn't return during the story. "But then, her fiancé died in a terrible accident."

"We've watched her through every stage of grief," the other friend continued.

"And honestly, we never really thought she'd make it through. There were some terribly dark times," the first friend said.

"But we never could have planned for Ned."

"Ned and Brittany are perfect for each other."

"Anyway. Sorry for spilling the beans on that story," the other friend said, giggling. "We're just over the moon for Brittany. And being here at the Pink Horsey..."

"Pony!" the other friend corrected, giggling.

"Sorry. The Pinky Pony..." The friend wrinkled her nose, then cackled. "It's just all been so wonderful."

Marcy's heart dripped into the acid of her stomach. "That's nice. I hope you continue to enjoy your day together." She then poured the contents of the champagne bottle into all three glasses and fled back inside, where the football fans howled at the television. Marcy's eyes were blurry with tears. *Why?* Why was she crying? She felt she'd lost all contact with her emotional center.

As she poured beers for another table of football fans, Marcy returned to a topic of thought that she normally liked to avoid. "Second chances." Throughout her twenties and into her thirties and forties, many people around the island questioned her about her dating life. "It's never too late to find the one," an older woman had coaxed so easily, as though she'd talked about the weather. Always, Marcy had been resistant. She'd had her "one." Why on earth would she go out and find another? *And wasn't it all just a big, stupid waste of time— especially considering the uncertain horror of what happened next?*

Yet here, this bride-to-be wore a silly sash and celebrated her "second chance" with some guy called "Ned." Should Marcy have followed that path? Should she have pushed herself to find her "Ned"? She shivered at the thought, knowing that nobody could have replaced Zane. It was far better that she'd kept to herself. She'd transformed herself into a powerful runner. She'd read more books than anyone else she knew. And on top of it all, she ran a very successful business, one that seemed more profitable by the day. Why would she want to share that life with anyone?

"Hey, Kurt?" Marcy called as she raced back behind the bar, having delivered another round of drinks. "You want a shot?"

Kurt wagged his eyebrows playfully. It was a rare thing that Marcy suggested that they drink on the job.

"What's the occasion?" Kurt asked.

"There isn't any. I just feel like it," Marcy returned as she planted both shot glasses on the counter and poured tequila. A few seconds later, she and Kurt knocked their heads back as they took the shots, acting more like twenty-one-year-olds than fifty-six-year-olds. When they came up for air, Kurt's eyes glittered excitedly. "Another?" Marcy asked.

"You've lost your mind," Kurt returned as he scampered back to another table to take an order. "This woman has lost her mind!" He hollered it playfully to no one in particular.

By seven-thirty, Marcy had had two tequila shots and a few sips of wine. A tiny woman with a runner's body, she couldn't exactly hold her liquor, and she found herself telling more jokes, being more animated with the bar revelers, and giggling with Kurt. All the while, the bride-to-be and her friends drank outside, soon wrapping up in sweaters and sweatshirts to ward off the growing chill. Marcy did her best to avoid conversation with the table, as the bride-to-be seemed to resemble, for her, everything that she'd never been able to achieve. But when the bride's friend called her over to "take their photo," Marcy couldn't figure out a way to avoid it.

"All right. Everyone, say cheese," Marcy said, her voice half-sarcastic and slightly annoyed.

"No, no. Let's not say cheese," one of the friends said. "To Ned and Brittany's great adventure!"

Together, she and the other friend said the words, which hardly aligned together, as they'd drank too much champagne at that point. In the middle, Brittany hovered on the edge of tears and laughter.

But as they finished out the words, Marcy's shoulders dropped forward. Her knees knocked together terribly as her face crumpled with sorrow.

"I'm sorry," Marcy stuttered, moving forward to return the phone.

"Oh, honey. Are you feeling okay?" Brittany began.

But already, Marcy scampered away from the table, knowing that she had to get out of there as quickly as she could, or else she would reveal herself to be a blubbering idiot in front of the entire bar. She rushed toward the staircase and hurried upstairs to the apartment she'd been raised in and collapsed at the kitchen table. Above the table, a photograph still hung of herself and Elliott— she, age fourteen, and he in his forties, younger than she was now.

"Marcy? Are you okay?" Kurt's voice hummed outside the door.

Marcy heaved a sigh and told herself to compose herself. She couldn't very well leave Kurt alone at the bar, not in this chaos. Slowly, she shifted to her feet and stumbled to the door, where she met Kurt with a large and false smile.

"Sorry about that," she said with a sniff.

Kurt's eyes were glassy. Down the staircase and through the bar, tourists howled with growing excitement. It was Saturday night by that point; they were taking that as a sign to live out their wildest fantasies, to drink all the drinks and eat all the fatty foods they pleased. Marcy's heart banged with resentment for them. All she wanted, just then, was to be left alone.

"We're going to take it easy tonight," Kurt said firmly. "We'll tell everyone we close by ten-thirty."

"That's not possible, Kurt."

"Why the heck not?" Kurt demanded. "You own this bar. You make the rules."

Marcy's tongue was dry and scaly, and her legs screamed from all the rushing around. Downstairs, one football team or another made a goal, and several people within the bar shrieked. It was difficult to say if their shrieks were good or bad.

"Okay," Marcy finally breathed. "All right. Ten-thirty, everyone has to be out."

It wasn't difficult to adjust the rules. At nine-forty-five, Kurt and Marcy called "last call" and said that they had to clean everything up early that night. As there were other bars along the road, all of which sold drinks till midnight, the silly partiers just moseyed up or down the cobblestones. This left Kurt and Marcy in the soft glow of the television, exhausted and heavy with tips paid in cash.

Kurt pointed toward the bar stool in front of the counter, snapped his fingers, and said, "Sit. Now." He then turned back, poured a large glass of water from the tap, and set the glass of water in front of Marcy. "Drink." Afterward, he ordered them two baskets of chicken wings from the kitchen, along with a big bucket of fries. When they finished the greasy explosion, he poured them two fingers each of Four Roses whiskey and said, "Penny for your thoughts?"

Marcy's throat swelled with a mix of sorrow and gratefulness. How could she possibly describe to Kurt just how much he meant to her? How could she explain to him that seeing so many brides everywhere had turned her blue without sounding like the most pathetic woman in the world? She lifted her whiskey glass and took a small sip, allowing the harsh liquid to burn her tongue. Just when she'd assumed that she didn't have the strength to say anything at all, she heard herself mutter, "I sometimes wonder if I made a mistake, staying here all that time after Zane..."

At the mention of Zane's name, Kurt's face grew stony. He sipped the whiskey and eyed the counter between them, recognizing the seriousness of the situation.

"I just can't help but imagine all these other lives I could have lived," Marcy continued to blabber. "Maybe I could have gone to Florida or California or Tennessee. Maybe I could have been something more than the owner of the Pink Pony. Maybe I could have known something more besides Mackinac Island."

Kurt selected a French fry from the bucket and chewed contemplatively from the edge. "Have you been feeling like this for a while now?"

Marcy shook her head. "The summer months are too frantic for too much thinking."

"It could be the chillier months. They're beautiful, but they always bring a bit of malaise. You know that."

Marcy's cheeks fell toward the ground. Just then, she felt far older than her fifty-six years. "It's not the weather. It's just me. It's just the decisions I've made."

Kurt and Marcy held the silence for a long time. Kurt, who ordinarily knew precisely what to say to cheer Marcy up, now seemed at a loss. He tossed the waste into the trashcan, ate several more fries, and then began to scrub the tables around the bar, still wordless. After a few moments, Marcy joined him, grateful to find solace in action rather than moping.

But after Marcy had cleaned three tables, she spun on her heel and said, "But haven't you ever regretted not leaving?"

Kurt lifted his chin and blinked at her. He seemed unwilling or unable to dive into this topic of conversation, but Marcy pushed it.

"I mean, you used to talk about all the lives you wanted to live," Marcy reminded him. "You told me that being captain at Shepler's was only the first step of the rest of your wild life."

All the color drained from Kurt's cheeks. Slowly, he folded the washcloth in his hands and marched back behind the counter. Marcy's words continued to echo between them, a consistent reminder that nothing had gone as planned in either of their lives.

"I just don't want to pretend that I'm living the life of my dreams anymore," Marcy continued, pressing the flat of her hand against her forehead. She felt absolutely insane.

Behind the counter, Kurt snapped off the computer system and turned the majority of the lights out. Marcy now stood in the bar like a shadow.

"I can't talk to you about this, Marcy," Kurt said finally, his voice soft yet firm. "I'm sorry. I really wish I could."

With that, Kurt collected his autumn jacket, slung it over his shoulders, and headed for the front door of the bar. Within seconds, he'd joined the frenetic chaos of one of the final gorgeous nights of the year, leaving Marcy alone, yet again, at the bar that had been her prison for the better part of forty years. There still seemed no way to escape.

Chapter Five

Alex Swartz managed most of Dean Swartz's holiday properties across Mackinac Island, which included a number of bed and breakfasts, hotels, full homes, and gorgeous apartments. For this reason, Elise had approached him a number of months ago about the potential to purchase a house on Mackinac Island, one that could become a forever home for her and Wayne. With Alex at the reins, the process of finding that "forever home" hadn't exactly been a grueling one, and already, early that October, Alex sat Wayne and Elise down with the final paperwork to purchase that very home— a gorgeous three-story Victorian about one block away from Dean and Cindy's homes.

"As you both know, the only caveat with this beautiful house is that it needs a great deal of work," Alex said as he snapped the end of his pen. "The old owners used to take care of it very well, as they were frequent summertime guests on the island. Over the years, they neglected their lives here and visited less and less. Now, only one of the owners remains alive in a nursing home just outside of Los Angeles. Needless to say, he won't be coming to Mackinac any time soon to fix up the space."

Elise and Wayne glanced at one another, both excited by the prospect of a "Fixer-Upper." This meant that they could make the space their own.

"The house is incredible," Elise said, flashing her half-brother a smile. "It's where we want to spend the next half of our lives."

Alex puffed out his cheeks and laughed. "Well, let me know if you need an extra set of hands. Working for all these bed and breakfasts and hotels has made me handier than I look."

"We'll count on that," Wayne said, whipping his hand forward to shake Alex's.

The old set of keys dangled in Elise's hand as she and Wayne headed up to the Pontiac Trail Head. The air was crisp, about fifty-two degrees, and the island's trees were now increasingly ostentatious, presenting a wide array of reds, oranges, and yellows.

"I never imagined that I'd move up to Pontiac Trail Head," Wayne said with a laugh. "What kind of man am I? I'm getting too big for my britches."

With a quick rush of energy, Elise pressed Wayne against a tree trunk and lifted her chin so that their nose met. Wayne laughed, surprised at her sudden playfulness and spontaneity.

After she kissed him, Elise breathed, "That house is something special. It would be silly of us to let it pass by."

Wayne grimaced. "I know that."

There was a moment of silence. Elise's shoulders sagged slightly.

"I know that it'll be hard for you to leave your place," she whispered.

Wayne gripped Elise's wrist tenderly. "But you're right. It's time for me to go."

Wayne had lived in his little one-story home with his first wife, Tara. Years ago, Tara had died in a car accident off the island, which had cast Wayne into an aimless search for happiness in the form of a "bad boy" lifestyle. When he'd met Elise, all of that had fallen away, and he'd been forced to ask himself tough questions about his own happiness.

Now, moving to a different space was the next step. But Elise had to appreciate how difficult it was for him to leave a world he'd once inhabited with his first love. (She'd had a first love, too. Although Sean had cheated on her, she still remembered the good times— and selling the place they'd shared in Calabasas had nearly shattered her heart. She understood a good amount of what Wayne was going through. She really did.)

The Victorian home they'd purchased looked like something out of a horror movie. The pillars on the wrap-around porch looked likely to give in at any moment. The paint was chipped; the windows were shutterless; and the garden was long overgrown, with trees and bushes whipping out of the dirt every-which-way.

"This place must have really been something special back in the day," Wayne muttered as he stepped forward, inching through the overgrown bushes to get to the front porch.

"It's going to be something special again soon," Elise called from behind him.

Wayne turned, his eyes glittering. "Let's open the door together."

Elise scampered forward and stood in front of the door handle, gripping the key. Wayne wrapped his warm hand around hers and slowly shoved the key into the lock, then turned her tiny hand so that the door creaked forward.

"Home sweet home," Wayne joked as they stepped into the chaos.

The owner out in Los Angeles had had all of the furniture

taken out and sold in auction. This left the bare bones of the house below, including a beautiful hardwood floor and white, barren walls. The kitchen counters and cabinets were bent from the watery air, and several steps leading to the second and third floors were busted. There were rumors of teenagers using the house as a sort of "party area," although there were no real signs of that. It just looked like a house worn from time.

Elise stood in the foyer and listened as the October wind tore against the house. The old bones of the house creaked around her, saying hello. Wayne stepped up behind her, wrapped his arms around her waist, and swayed with her, wordless. Both were overcome with the immensity of their mission— that and the power of the destiny that they'd decided to build together. Elise had decided long ago not to allow "destiny" to have its way with her. Instead, she would call the shots on where her career went, who she chose to love, and how she would live. It was an invigorating feeling.

They wandered into the kitchen, where Wayne procured a bottle of champagne from a backpack and uncorked it. The froth curled around the lip of the bottle. Wayne's eyes caught Elise's, heavy with excitement and love. As he poured them both glasses (which he'd also brought in his backpack), Elise closed her eyes and imagined a day, perhaps one year from now, or perhaps two, when they would host Cindy, Tracey, Dean, Alex, Penny, Brad, Emma, and Megan. She imagined them around a table on the front porch, cackling as the sun bent low over the Straits of Mackinac. She imagined the soul-affirming smells that wafted in from the kitchen— lemon chicken or salmon or pot pie. She imagined Cindy, Tracey, and Elise sharing a pot of tea as the rain blasted against the window-panes. "It's so cozy here," she imagined Cindy saying as she curled up on the gorgeous couch she would inevitably buy, one that would suit the space perfectly.

As a California girl, her newfound love for autumn and

winter was a strange one. She supposed that this was all based on genetics. Her father was Dean Swartz, after all— and Dean Swartz loved winters on Mackinac more than anyone she knew. He donned a flannel and a thick wool hat and was set till spring while the rest of the island shivered and moaned.

"To us," Wayne breathed, lifting his glass of champagne toward her.

"To us," Elise whispered back, her voice breaking. They clinked glasses and sipped. Another gust surged into the house, threatening to shatter the remaining glass in the windows. Both giggled, eyes widening. "We have our work cut out for us."

"I can see it in your eyes. You've already got a plan for most of the rooms in the house," Wayne teased.

Elise blushed. "Nothing is finalized. I've just been dreaming."

"That creative mind of yours. You can't turn it off!"

Elise giggled and scampered out of the kitchen, heading for the staircase with her glass of champagne still lifted. Slowly, she walked up the steps, careful to only shift her weight onto the wooden slabs that could handle her. Down below, Wayne asked, "Where do you think you're going?"

"We've hardly seen the upstairs," Elise countered, her eyes flashing back to meet his. "I want to see what the bedroom looks like!"

Wayne laughed and began his ascent, making sure to take the same steps that Elise had already taken. When they reached the second story, they tip-toed across the landing and peered into all three bedrooms and the dilapidated bathroom, which probably required "a real professional."

But their bedroom was exquisite. A large bay window faced the Straits of Mackinac, which now frothed beneath the angry October winds. The hardwood floors were slightly warped but mostly okay, and an old floral wallpaper remained, reminiscent of the forties or fifties. Elise stepped in, feeling a part of someone else's dreams.

"It's hard to believe that the family who owned this only came here for summers," Elise said, touching the wallpaper lightly. "Who could resist being here full-time?"

"Not everyone can run away from their lives the way you can," Wayne pointed out. "People have responsibilities that have nothing to do with the island."

"That sounds just terrible," Elise said playfully.

When she reached the center of the wall opposite the bay window, she wrapped her hand around the golden knob of a closet and slowly pulled it open. The closet itself was enormous, with enough space on either wall for both Wayne and Elise to double their wardrobes. Elise reminded Wayne that he'd already promised that one of the spare bedrooms could be her wardrobe slash writing office, which would allow him to use the walk-in closet more often if he wanted that.

"Are you suggesting that I should go shopping? I don't have enough clothes for this," Wayne quipped.

Elise laughed. "You're just like my father. All you need is a flannel shirt and a pair of jeans. Where's the style in your life? Where's the creativity?"

Wayne rolled his eyes and said, "You don't want me to step up my fashion game, Elise. You'd fall out of the spotlight immediately. The way we do things right now, everyone can focus on your pretty skirts and your beautiful hair and those little sweaters you wear."

Elise blushed, falling against him like an amorous teenage girl. "You know, complimenting me won't get you out of every argument."

"I don't know what you mean," Wayne joked with a twinkle in his eye.

After another kiss, Wayne lifted his chin to point toward something in the closet. "What's that about?"

Elise turned and peered through the shadows to discover a large trunk tucked into the corner of the closet. "Huh. That's weird. Alex said the old owner got rid of everything." The door screamed as she opened it wider, stepping through to drop down on the hardwood and fiddle with the lock around the opening of the trunk. Miraculously, it opened.

"Uh oh," Elise said, feigning breathlessness. "Is this the part of the movie where we discover treasure?"

"I'll be your Indiana Jones, baby," Wayne quipped.

Elise cackled as she removed the lock, dropping it beside her as she heaved the trunk open. Dust barrelled out of the opening, and she coughed, turning her head.

"Careful!" Wayne sounded worried. He stepped through the shadows to lean down beside her, his hand on her shoulder. "You good?"

Elise coughed once more and nodded. "I'm really okay."

"We shouldn't be going through old stuff like this. There could be mold or bugs or..."

"Where's your sense of adventure, Wayne?"

Wayne waved a hand through the dissipating dust, grabbed his phone, and flashed the light from it into the trunk. "Looks like a bunch of junk."

Mostly, it was. Elise leafed through the first several layers, discovering old diaries that had been water-damaged, old books that were probably worth a pretty penny (Elise stacked them and planned to speak to her antiquarian friend later), and several photo albums filled with strange faces.

"Birthday parties. Weddings. Picnics on the beach..." Elise muttered as she flipped through the pages, which were mostly unlabelled. "It's so surreal to peer back at other people's memories. Someone took these photos for a reason! I wonder where those people are now."

Wayne continued to piece through the trunk, clearly interested. "What do you think we should do with all of it?"

"I don't know. It doesn't feel like it's up to us to do anything with it," Elise breathed.

Wayne lifted his shoulder. "I've seen photo albums at second-hand stores before. I always wonder, who brought this here? Who gave up on their memories?"

Elise's heart felt tweaked with sorrow. For a long moment, she studied an old photograph of another birthday party scene in which a three- or four-year-old boy sat at a table with cake smeared across his cheeks. The photo was black and white, yet it still echoed the magic of a beautiful summer's day long ago.

"Oh, woah. What is this?" Wayne lifted a large cylinder from within the trunk. The cylinder had little tin protectants on either side, one of which Wayne popped out so that he could peer in.

Very carefully, Elise and Wayne shifted the piece of paper within the cylinder and splayed it across the bedroom floor. The paper was decades old, clearly, but hadn't seen much sunlight or wet air and was in rather good shape.

"They're blueprints," Wayne muttered, placing an old diary at one corner of the paper to make sure it didn't curl up again. "For what seems to be an elaborate home."

Wayne was right. Together, Elise and Wayne explored the make-believe home— the first floor with its enormous kitchen, the wrap-around porch, the multi-leveled living room, the parlor, the upstairs four bedrooms, and the third floor's "library." There were two staircases, both of which wrapped in circles like in an old fairy-tale house, and there were even a few "hidden passageways" in the blueprints, proof that whoever had designed this had wanted to be personal and playful with it.

"Do you think this house exists anywhere?" Elise asked, captivated by the image she'd created in her mind from the blueprints.

Wayne continued to scour the tiny print along the edge of

the blueprints, taking stock of things Elise couldn't understand and never planned to.

"Looks like there are coordinates," Wayne said suddenly, his finger stabbing the hardwood directly beside the tiny numbers. When he lifted his eyes toward Elise's, they glittered with intrigue and promise.

"Looks like someone has turned into Indiana Jones, after all," Elise said, her smile widening.

Wayne rolled his eyes but beamed, clearly pleased with himself. He grabbed his phone and typed in the coordinates, talking about a course he'd once taken online about architecture plans and how he'd "always dreamed" of designing his own space. Midway through his description of the class, however, his eyes widened with shock.

"The coordinates loaded," he said.

"And? Where is this beautiful house?" Elise asked.

Wayne turned his phone around to show the map. Elise gasped. The coordinates led to somewhere not far from the very house they now sat in, tucked into the woods— presumably with a beautiful view of the Straits of Mackinac beyond.

"Is this house back there?" Elise demanded, searching her own mind map of Mackinac.

Wayne clucked his tongue. "No. There's no house like that back there."

Elise rushed to her feet, enthralled. Outside, the wind had calmed the slightest bit, allowing a later-afternoon hazy blue to bleed out across the sky. "Let's walk up there. Just to see."

"I'm telling you, Elise," Wayne said with a laugh. "There's no house up there. It's just woods."

Elise groaned. "Come on, Wayne. I just want to go up there and visualize what it might have been like."

"You writers and your imagination." Wayne grumbled playfully as he slowly rolled back up the blueprints and tucked them back into the protector. "But after that, I suggest we head back to the house, make some chili, and get some rest."

"Sounds good to me."

Elise and Wayne slid back into their autumn jackets, locked the door to the old house (their new home!), joined hands, and headed back around the Pontiac Trail Head and deep into the forest of Mackinac. The walk to reach the coordinates took no longer than fifteen minutes, during which their feet oozed through soft leaves and late-year mud. As the day was nearly over, they met no one else on the trail, which lent a "creepy" feeling to the walk. It felt almost as though they'd drifted off the Mackinac Island that they knew and into an eerie, otherworldly version.

When they reached the coordinates, Elise gasped with surprise.

There, just as Wayne had said, the forest continued on—trees bursting from the wet ground and wielding their leaves toward the dark blue sky. Directly at the coordinates, however, the trees were young and slender and spread apart, with little bushes at their bases. Further back from the coordinates, the trees were older and much thicker. It looked as though, once upon a time, the space had been cleared. *Had it been cleared for the very house from the blueprints?*

It seemed like too much of a coincidence.

Elise wandered through the younger trees, her eyes misting at the intrigue of it all.

"It's bizarre," Wayne said under his breath.

"How old do you think these trees are?" Elise asked.

"It's hard to say. Thirty years? Maybe a bit older?" Wayne said. "The forest has a masterful way of repairing itself. But you can really see that there was human involvement here."

Elise whipped around the trees, suddenly overcome with energy and excitement. Her arms around Wayne, she exhaled with, "This is the kind of mystery I want to sink my teeth into."

Wayne chuckled. "I don't know how in the world you'd begin to figure this one out. The trees are doing their best to take over, as though the blueprints never existed."

Elise shivered into laughter. "You're probably right. But that doesn't mean that I won't do all I can to try."

Chapter Six

1987

The seamstress who adjusted Marcy's wedding dress mere weeks before her wedding to Zane had been a long-time friend of Marcy's mother. For this reason, Brenda had told Marcy, without question, that she would be taking absolutely no money for the work. "Losing your mother was a tragedy," she'd said, her eyes shadowed. "The least I can do is make sure you're all ready for the next step in life. This wedding dress is a part of that. Gosh, your mother would have been so proud of you."

Now, Marcy stood in the final form of the wedding dress, with its poofy eighties-style sleeves, its glistening Cinderella-skirt, and its cinched waist, and allowed herself to feel the full weight of this moment. Brenda bustled around her, inspecting the way the dress fit, before sniffing, "I think it looks just perfect on you, honey. Just perfect. Oh, but what wouldn't?

You're twenty-one years old, on the brink of the rest of your life. You'd look beautiful in a pillowcase."

Marcy laughed, her stomach tightening within the fabric. When she turned to catch Brenda's eye, her own were filled with tears, and the world around her began to blur. She opened her lips to attempt to describe just what this meant to her. But instead, Brenda placed her hand tenderly on Marcy's and whispered, "I know, darling. I know." Marcy was grateful for this. It was increasingly difficult for her to find the appropriate words to tell anyone how she truly felt.

Brenda had agreed to keep the dress in the safety of her own closet until the wedding day. Marcy slipped out of the dress and donned a pair of jean shorts and a tank top, puffing up her curly hair as Brenda chatted to her about her husband and his recent assertion that they move to Florida. "He can't take the cold anymore. The arthritis is getting too bad."

"I'd hate to see you go," Marcy said before turning her smile to the ground and adding, "Although it's looking more and more like Zane and I will be moving to Seattle."

Brenda's face broke into a gorgeous smile, one that echoed youth and vitality. "You're kidding. Seattle?"

Marcy squeezed her eyes shut and shrieked joyously. "He's out there right now doing a final round of interviews. I can hardly believe it. I mean, I know he's a very talented architect and deserving of every accolade and accomplishment. It's just incredible to me that this time, I'll get to go with him."

"You sure will, honey." At this, Brenda's eyes formed slits as she whispered, "And your daddy? Does he know?"

Marcy's heart dropped. Her father's volatility was island gossip, just as well-known as the weather. "Zane says that we can spend most summers here," she explained timidly. "We have plans to make sure we won't lose all connection to Mackinac." What she actually meant, of course, was that they wouldn't lose all connection to her father.

But in a flash, Brenda waved her hand knowingly and said, "You had better send me postcards from Seattle when I get down to Florida. I'll be whiling away in the heat while you're climbing up and down snow-topped mountains. What a marvelous life we'll both be living! Oh, but how I'll miss Mackinac."

"Mackinac will always have our hearts," Marcy agreed.

* * *

A half-hour later, Marcy met Kurt at the little sandwich café near the ferry docks. Kurt had worked tirelessly that early morning and afternoon, ultimately going forward and back on the Straits twelve times. As it was mid-July, his forehead and cheeks were red with the sun, and his eyes were relaxed and easy, concentrating on Marcy joyously as she described to him how it had felt to wear the fitted wedding dress.

Kurt spoke eagerly about an upcoming interview he had with Walt Disney World. "They said that I could be in charge of a small division in tourism management," he explained, his eyes sparkling. "I mean, Disney World is next level. The money is there. The people are lovely. And besides that, no winters. Can you imagine?"

Marcy laughed. "I never took you for a Disney guy."

"It's not that I'm a Disney guy," Kurt said, blushing in a way that made his red cheeks still redder. "But I told you already that I want to travel the world. If my experience in hospitality can help me get out into the world, I'll take it. Next stop, Orlando."

Marcy tossed her head back joyously. "I'm waiting on a call tonight from Zane. He's in the final interview for this architecture firm in Seattle."

"Seattle!" Kurt looked vaguely stricken for a moment but soon rebounded. He smacked his palms across his thigh and said, "Look at us, Marcy! We're on the brink of the rest of our lives."

"I guess we'd better appreciate the good times," Marcy joked, eyeing the sandwiches between them, the steady clopping of the horse and buggies along the cobblestone roads, and the beautiful Midwestern sun above. "I wonder if we'll ever look back at these days and wish we could have them back?"

Kurt waved a hand. "It's better not to think that way. By then, we'll have so much money and so many accolades that it won't matter."

Marcy snorted. Conspiratorially, she added, "Now that Zane is off to the races on his career, it's my turn to figure out what I want. Imagine me as someone who isn't a bartender. Someone who can do something else besides pour a beer?"

Kurt snapped his fingers. "Don't sell yourself short. You pour a near-perfect beer."

"You're a funny man, Kurt." Marcy rolled her eyes.

"Marcy!" A voice rang out through the streets of downtown Mackinac. Marcy lifted her eyes to watch as her father's friend, Vic, rushed toward her, his knees lifting as he sprinted. His face was stricken.

Immediately, a million terrible ideas sprung to Marcy's mind. Maybe, something was wrong with her father. All that stress had finally gotten to him. Marcy leaped to her feet, her hand on her chest.

"Vic? What's wrong?" Marcy couldn't recognize her own voice.

Vic stopped short at the table, sputtering, on the hunt for air. He stared at the ground beneath them, searching for an explanation. Kurt leaped to his feet and placed his hand on Vic's shoulder, saying, "You okay, Vic? Drink this water. Please."

Vic took Kurt's water, tossed a large portion down his throat, and finally said, "Your dad. He—"

Marcy fell to the chair beneath her, panicked. Her legs could no longer support her. Vic took another big swig of water, then finally said, "It's not what you think." His eyes were beady. "He was drunk...is drunk. A guy at the Pink Pony got under his skin. He punched him a new one, and Bobby at the police station came down and took him in. He's waiting on bail now."

In a split-second, Marcy shot from unnatural fear and sorrow to absolute anger. She leaped to her feet again, staring at Vic as though he was the devil himself. "Who did he punch?"

"Just some tourist," Vic explained, now cowering in front of Marcy.

"This is ridiculous. Ridiculous!" Marcy howled with her hands in fists. She stomped around the table, grabbing her purse as she went. "I asked for one afternoon off so that I can get my wedding dress fitted. And this is what he decides to do?" She was on a tirade at this point, mostly speaking to herself.

"But wait! Marcy?" Vic stumbled toward her, showing now that he, too, was a bit tipsy. Probably, he and her father had been drinking together, even as Elliott was meant to be manning the bar. "He said to tell you to take over the bar rather than pay off his bail. He can sleep it off at the police station."

Marcy's nostrils flared. With an enormous wave of rage, she spun toward Vic and howled, "I know that, Vic. I know. You think that I would just let the Pink Pony close for the day because of my father's stupidity?" She then leaped toward the sidewalk and hustled toward the Pink Pony, where already a stream of tourists lined up outside the door.

"Marcy! Hey!" Kurt rushed up behind her, gasping for air. "Wait up!"

But Marcy didn't have time to wait up. She continued to snap her feet forward, enraged. She was terrified that her father's anger could get the better of him so easily. Even more than that, however, she was terrified about leaving him behind on Mackinac. *Could he actually handle himself alone?* And what would he say when she told him she was moving to Seattle? *Would he fly into another fiery rage?* Would he choose to punch her instead? He'd never been specifically violent toward her, but Marcy couldn't rule it out.

All this played in contrast to the fact that Marcy knew, beyond a shadow of a doubt, that her father loved her more than he loved any creature on earth. It was a conundrum.

When Marcy reached the throng of tourists, she lifted her pale palms toward the sky and called out, "All right, everyone! I'm here to take your drink orders. Please, be patient with me."

Twenty pairs of eyes landed on Marcy expectantly. Slowly, she pierced the thick crowd and entered the bar's welcome shadow. In a flash, she was behind the bar counter, pouring beer after beer, digging through the refrigerator for bottles of white wine, and telling a few locals that she "didn't have time" to make them any complicated cocktails. (Obviously, if tourists from out of town wanted a cocktail, she would make that.)

"I got that wine order, Marcy." A familiar voice rang out beside her. Marcy turned to find that Kurt had barrelled through the tourists as well and now was hunkered behind the bar, grabbing a fresh bottle of wine from the large fridge. "You focus on the beers."

Marcy stuttered. "Kurt, you don't have to do this. You were up at four o'clock this morning."

But Kurt just waved a hand. "Pour the beers, Marcy. I can handle it. I got you."

Together, Marcy and Kurt dove through the terror of a beautiful afternoon at a bar on Mackinac Island. Between big rushes of tourists, Marcy taught Kurt how to work the register, which allowed him to print receipts, put orders into the machine, and take money. Hour after hour passed with hardly a moment's peace.

When they finally kicked the final tourist out at twelve-thirty that night, Marcy flipped the CLOSED sign out on the glass door and fell to her knees on the sticky ground. Behind the bar, Kurt wailed, "We did it!" He then placed a tape in the tape player and began to play Survivor's "Eye of the Tiger," which made Marcy wallop with laughter. She forced herself up, cackling as she raced back behind the bar and poured them each a shot of tequila. With tears streaming down her cheeks, she wailed, "I could never have done that without you. How did I get so lucky?"

Kurt clinked his shot glass with hers, closed his eyes, and said, "We got through that by the seat of our pants." They drank the shots, their tongues fizzing with the alcohol, and then immediately called over to the pizza place a few doors down, which had just closed its doors for the night. The guy behind the counter agreed to trade them pizza for beer, which Marcy welcomed.

"We've been so slammed tonight. We haven't eaten at all," she explained.

Very soon after, Marcy and Kurt sat on the floor of the upstairs apartment, where Marcy and Elliott lived alone. Between them sat a cardboard box filled with gooey, cheesy pizza layered with vegetables, sausages, and ham. Marcy ate with her eyes half-opened, slowly inching back to life.

"I guess I'll go collect my dad in the morning," she said softly. It was the first time she'd allowed herself to think of him, probably stretched out on a bench at the police station.

Kurt groaned. "You want me to come with you?"

Marcy shook her head. "Naw. I don't want you to have to experience his wrath. Not after all you did tonight."

"He can be sweet," Kurt offered.

"Yeah. But not when he's hungover after a night at the station," Marcy said, grimacing.

Kurt placed his half-eaten slice of pizza on the box and stared at the ground. He seemed on the verge of saying something. Instead of waiting for whatever that was, Marcy leaped to her feet and headed for the fridge.

"You want another beer? I sure as heck do."

"Yeah. Okay." Kurt sounded resistant.

Once in the kitchen, Marcy hunted through the fridge, grabbed two cans of beer, and turned around. En route to the living room, the phone on the wall blared. Every cell in her body froze with fear. *Who could be calling at this hour?*

The only answer came a split-second later. It had to be Zane, who was still out in Seattle and, therefore, three hours behind in time. It was still rather early there.

"Good evening, stranger." Zane's voice was cool as a cucumber, deep and welcoming.

"Zane!" Marcy cooed as she twirled the phone line around her finger.

In the next room, Kurt grabbed his half-eaten slice of pizza and began to shove it down his throat. Marcy watched him yet couldn't pull herself fully from Zane's voice. Oh, how she wished they were already married. Oh, how she wished that he would take her away from all this.

"I wanted to call you as soon as I knew," Zane said. "I've been out with my new boss all night. He offered me the job. It's really happening, baby. We're moving to Seattle."

Marcy closed her eyes and swooned against the wall. Immediately, a vision of her future flashed before her eyes— gorgeous pictures of her and Zane in Seattle, hiking mountains with their children and swimming in glistening, blue streams. Could that future really belong to her? Days like this day would be only memories.

"That's such good news, Zane," Marcy whispered, overwhelmed. "I love you so much. I can't wait to start our life together."

"I know, baby. I love you, too."

Chapter Seven

Present Day

Elise was having computer problems. Outside, a wind thrust itself against the windows of her and Wayne's little house, and the internet shimmered in and out—making her correspondence with Malcolm, the director of the movie she'd written (and the potential love of Tracey's life) very difficult. Again, she heaved a sigh, clicked the video chat icon, and finally heard the ringtone that meant she was calling California. She and Malcolm just needed to talk for a few more minutes, and then she would be off for the weekend. She was anxious to get back out to the home she and Wayne had purchased, if only to dig through that trunk and get to work on discovering the secrets of the old place. *Who did the blueprints belong to? Who had given up on that glorious dream?*

"Hi! There you are again," Elise said, smiling at the video

image of the handsome director. "Oh gosh, all that sun out the window is making my heart hurt for California."

Malcolm laughed good-naturedly. "It's eighty-five degrees and humid. I don't think you want that."

"Why don't you come out to Mackinac, then?" Elise said. "I know someone out here who wouldn't mind seeing you again."

Malcolm's cheeks were blotchy with embarrassment. He palmed the back of his neck, then added, "I just bought my flight to Detroit. I can't wait for that wedding of yours. It'll be the first celebration of sorts that I've had in many years. Since my daughter's diagnosis and the divorce and then the endless fight to get back into the directing business, I haven't made much time for 'fun.'" He put air quotes around that last word.

"We will be so happy to welcome you back to the island!" Elise said. "Hard to believe it's only about two weeks away."

"Enjoy every second," Malcolm warned her. "It'll go by quickly."

Elise was reminded of what she'd already told Michael about his time with his brand-new baby. Time was precious. You had to pay attention to it.

After Elise's meeting with Malcolm, she jotted several notes to herself on a notepad, stood up, stretched her hands to her toes, and then heard the front bell ring. This was curious, as she hadn't expected Wayne for at least two more hours— and it wasn't like him to ring the doorbell.

Elise hustled out of the little office she'd cultivated for her writing and headed for the front door. As she went, another huge gust of wind rammed against the house. A shiver raced up and down her spine.

When Elise opened the door, her jaw dropped with surprise. There, shivering on the front porch next to a rolling suitcase, all bundled up in winter garb, was Elise's darling daughter, Penny. Her cheeks were tinged red with cold, and her eyes shimmered with tears and excitement. Like Elise,

Penny was a California girl, through and through— and the Mackinac autumn was a test of her strength.

Yet, here she was, so far from home.

"Darling!" Elise flung forward, wrapping her arms around her daughter.

"Mom, it's so, so cold." Penny spoke into Elise's shoulder.

"Get in here." Elise heaved her daughter over the threshold, making Penny shiver even more with laughter. With Penny safely in the foyer, Elise grabbed Penny's suitcase and placed it delicately on the hardwood of the foyer. Then, she thrust the door closed just as another chilly gust of wind tore through.

Penny gasped with another round of laughter and slowly rotated the scarf from her neck. "You've got to be kidding me! One winter in Mackinac is 'quaint.' But two? You have to be out of your mind."

Elise dropped her head back, ecstatic over the sound of her daughter's voice, bouncing from wall to wall. Like Penny's grandmother before her, Penny was a very talented actress. Unlike Penny's grandmother, Penny had had a smattering of roles already throughout her time at the University of California, Berkeley. Now, she was on the hunt for theater and film roles, taking frequent auditions and speaking conspiratorially about returning to Los Angeles for good. All of this, Elise normally heard over the phone from thousands of miles across the continent.

"Tell me," Elise said, guiding her daughter into the kitchen. "To what do I owe this surprise?" At the kitchen stove, she snapped on the burner beneath the tea kettle and rubbed her palms together, taking in the splendorous view of her beautiful daughter.

Penny tilted her head knowingly, her smile secretive. "Are you suggesting that I would miss out on your bachelorette party?"

Elise's eyebrows popped toward her hairline. "Bachelorette party?"

Suddenly, the doorbell rang again. Penny clapped her hands joyously and hollered, "Let the games begin!" Elise hustled out toward the foyer just as the kettle's water began to simmer. When she opened the door, she discovered Tracey and Emma all bundled up and smiling.

"There she is. Our bride-to-be!" Tracey howled as she rushed forward to hug Elise.

Emma, who'd just discovered she was pregnant a couple of months before, still hardly showed. The only proof of her pregnancy was in the glow of her skin and the optimism in her smile. She hugged Elise as well and watched as her mother pranced around the room animatedly, talking about a recent client who'd just purchased four hundred dollars worth of inventory at her little shop downtown.

"She couldn't make up her mind," Tracey said, her chest heaving. "She tried on nearly every item in the shop. I thought she would never leave, Elise! Imagine that I'd have to miss the start of your bachelorette party, all because of this woman's inability to choose turquoise over lime green!"

Elise cackled just as another ring of the bell buzzed through the house. "I wonder who that could be?" She opened it to find, of course, Cindy, Megan, and, to her surprise, Margot, Michael's girlfriend, whom he'd met in Texas. Elise had hardly seen Margot since the baby had been born. Much like Michael, Margot wore large bags beneath her eyes, and her hair was wild and unkempt. Still, much like all new parents, she seemed overwhelmed with love and newfound responsibility— and spoke quickly and excitedly, grateful to be included in her new family's festivities.

"I told Michael that I just couldn't wait for a night out with the girls again," Margot said, swinging her Texan accent around. "I'm still new on this little island of yours, and I have to admit— having a baby doesn't do wonders for your social life."

Cindy, Tracy, and Elise all nodded knowingly. Emma grimaced and squeezed Margot's wrist. "I'll be right there with you in no time."

Margot's eyes glittered. "I know that neither of our pregnancies was planned, but goodness me, what timing! Our babies will grow up together. They'll be the greatest of friends."

"Elise? Do you have everything? Your coat? Your purse?" Cindy spoke earnestly.

"I don't know what I need! Nobody told me any of this was happening," Elise said.

"First, I reckon we need a round of drinks!" Margot said, hunting through her backpack to find two bottles of champagne. "Just to get this party started."

With a flourish, Margot yanked the first cork from the champagne bottle and lined her hand with bubbles. Tracey cried, "Oompa!" as Cindy reminded all of them that "the carriage would arrive within the next half-hour."

"Carriage? Who am I, Cinderella?" Elise joked, her smile widening.

"Just get home before midnight, Cinderella," Tracey teased with a wink.

Hurriedly, Megan and Margot poured them all glasses of champagne and passed them around in the kitchen. Penny played music from Elise's "golden era," the nineties, while Tracey lifted her glass toward the light and said, "To a weekend none of us will ever forget."

"An entire weekend? You're spoiling me!" Elise cried.

"Mom, just let us spoil you!" Penny quipped. "You've worked yourself silly the past several months. Isn't it time to start celebrating?"

Elise dropped her head onto her daughter's shoulder and

fell into the haze of love she felt for these beautiful people. She thanked them, and then she thanked them again. More champagne was poured just as Cindy reminded them that they needed to prepare for the carriage. Tracey checked the window to say that the wind had cleared a bit, which was a good thing, as their carriage ride was "on the longer side."

"Where on earth are you taking me?" Elise cried.

The answer came soon after.

Elise, Penny, Megan, Emma, Tracey, Cindy, and Margot loaded themselves up in a carriage, one upon which Kurt from Shepler's Mackinac Island Ferry sat in a thick winter coat. He greeted them warmly and congratulated Elise on her upcoming wedding. Elise thanked him and said, "I didn't know you were the captain of anything more than Shepler's Ferries."

"I like to think that I could be the captain of anything," Kurt joked. "Just give me the reins, and I'll take you wherever you want to go." His eyes opened wider with good humor as he added, "And when Tracey told me the other night that they were struggling to find a carriage driver for your bachelorette party, I just knew I had to step in."

"He saved the day," Tracey affirmed.

The Swartz women had rented a cabin on the eastern edge of the island, about ten minutes' walk from Arch Rock and in full view of the sweeping lake beyond. The cabin itself featured five rooms, a large living area with a working fireplace, cozy couches, a baby grand piano, and a complete kitchen, which had already been stocked with plenty of wine, champagne, healthy and not-so-healthy snacks, and vegetables, eggs, cheeses, and meats for breakfast. As Elise explored, her heart in her throat, Tracey explained that they would be doing "all of the heavy-lifting" when it came to things like cooking and cleaning and that, of course, they had other festivities planned throughout the weekend, including horseback riding, a wine tasting, and dinner at the Grand Hotel.

"Tonight, we have dinner reservations downtown," Tracey continued, her eyes shimmering. "And then back at the cabin, the wild games will begin."

"Wild games?" Elise shrieked, locking eyes with Penny.

"Mom, come on. It's your bachelorette. It can't be tame," Penny teased.

Cindy fetched a small cheese platter from the refrigerator, turned on the fireplace (which was a far cry from fireplaces of the past— requiring only an ON/OFF switch), poured another round of champagne, and turned on a bit of music. Over cheese, the women of the Swartz family chatted easily, switching conversation topics from Megan's recent months at Michigan State University, to Emma's pregnancy, to the recent drama of Emma's father's return (and very soon after, his abandonment), plus Elise's recent video calls with Malcolm, whom Tracey clearly missed a great deal.

"He's coming to the wedding," Elise reminded Tracey, arching her eyebrow.

Tracey blushed and dropped her gaze to her champagne glass. "I think it's better that I don't consider him as an option. We spent a beautiful few weeks together. Maybe it was never meant to be anything more than that."

Elise's heart felt bruised at the sentiment. Still, she knew what Tracey meant: not everything was supposed to last forever. You had to be grateful for the time that you had.

After another round of drinks, Tracey called Kurt back to pick them up and take them to dinner. Once at the downtown restaurant, Kurt explained that he had to rush over to the Pink Pony to assist Marcy with a big rush of tourists.

"We'll come find you when we're finished," Tracey said. "I'm sure we'll be in the mood for another drink at the Pony, anyway."

Kurt nodded knowingly, waved to Elise, and said, "Have a beautiful dinner, ladies."

The dinner was gorgeous: plump cuts of steak, ravioli with ricotta and spinach, salmon that oozed with lemon flavor, and pumpkin risotto. The wine flowed steadily as their conversation continued to flourish, digging into the beautiful details of the years that had come before, along with their expectations of what would come next. Elise understood that her decision to marry Wayne was a reason for everyone to celebrate, as it was proof that you could build brand-new eras for yourself. The past would always be the past, *but what was next for you?*

"Things have been just wonderful with Ron," Cindy said, twirling her fork through her spaghetti with clams. "It's strange to start over with someone new because it means learning a whole new set of rules and a whole new vocabulary. But then again, there was so much hatred between Fred and I at the end..."

Tracey nodded sadly and glanced toward Elise. To Elise, she felt that she and Tracey shared the same sentiment. They hated that Cindy had had to live with such an abusive man for so many decades; now, they were so grateful that he'd left the island for good, allowing Cindy the space to build a fresh life for herself. There was no telling what would happen next between Cindy and Ron. One thing was clear, though: Cindy deserved a second chance more than most people. Her heart had been ripped in two more than once.

After dinner, the women swept off into the chill of the night, walking the two blocks to the Pink Pony, which buzzed with Friday night traffic and glowed warmly from behind the large windows. Just as ever, the beautiful Marcy stood behind the bar, nodding along to whatever drivel the guys at the bar counter spoke. Television screens showed several different sporting events and even one black-and-white movie, while the speakers in the corners played Led Zeppelin tunes. Conveniently, Kurt had reserved the women a table in the corner and had even written: ELISE DARBY - BACHELORETTE PARTY in big block letters on a piece of paper.

"There they are!" Kurt greeted them warmly as he buzzed past. "How was dinner?"

The women said it was "to die for" before ordering the first round of cocktails and waving to Marcy behind the bar. Again, they fell into easy conversation in the corner, buzzing with adrenaline. Elise no longer remembered her age. She suddenly felt as exuberant and youthful as her daughter, Penny. She was on the brink of the rest of her life. Why shouldn't she feel anything but bliss?

As Elise sipped through the end of her first Moscow Mule, Marcy appeared beside her to collect Tracey and Penny's glasses. "There she is. The bachelorette!" Marcy said, giving Elise a half-smile.

Elise grinned. "It's all so silly, isn't it?"

Marcy clucked her tongue. "All we need in life is a reason to celebrate."

"That's right!" Elise lifted her glass joyously.

"Elise is all about big reasons to celebrate right now," Tracey continued. "She's finishing out the movie, she's getting married, her daughter's here from California, and she just bought a house!"

It was difficult to tell if Marcy feigned interest or not. "That's great news, Elise. It wouldn't do for you and Wayne to stay in that little house of his. You need something of your own."

"We thought the same thing." Elise cast Cindy a soft smile, knowing that Cindy's best friend in the world had been Tara, Wayne's first wife. "I know that it will be hard for Wayne to say goodbye to the old place. Luckily, he won't have to for a while since we bought a place that needs maybe an entire year of restorations."

"A year!" Marcy cackled appreciatively. "You always bite off more than you can chew, don't you?"

"That's what I told her," Penny said, faking anger. "She doesn't know how to rest."

Elise waved a hand. "We'll have plenty of help, I'm sure. Right now, we're trying to get our heads around the old place. I'm visualizing how I want the space to look. It's up near Cindy's and Dad's places, so it has plenty of light."

Suddenly, Marcy's face shifted and grew stony. Elise's smile faltered as she recognized the change.

"You got that old, abandoned place up near the Trail Head?" Marcy asked, tilting her head. Her tone was strange. Elise was sure that she'd never heard Marcy quite like this.

"That's the one," Elise replied. "The old Victorian."

"Huh. Never thought the old owners would sell it," Marcy muttered, still with that same tone.

"Did you know the old owners?" Elise asked.

Marcy clucked her tongue and collected Elise's now-empty glass. "Not well, no. Would you like another? As far as I know, bachelorette parties aren't meant to stay dry for long."

"Get her another one!" Tracey howled.

"I'll take that as an order," Marcy said, her tone returning to its bouncy playfulness. "Anyone else?"

Marcy took the rest of the table's orders and soon returned behind the bar to stir them up. Around them, tourists continued to banter and burst with laughter. Elise's own table bubbled with its own easy conversation, this time turning to Emma's insistence that she wouldn't date again until after her baby was much, much older.

"There's no reason to turn your back on love like that," Penny urged Emma. "People date and fall in love under all sorts of circumstances. You'll have a baby. So what? Plenty of people date with babies."

Emma grimaced. "It's just so messy."

"Everything is messy!" Megan reminded her.

Elise's gaze flickered back behind the bar, where Marcy stood quietly, stirring up another Moscow Mule. Elise's heart burned with curiosity. Why had Marcy been so strange about Elise's new house, "the old, abandoned place up near the Trail Head"? Yet again, Elise acknowledged that she knew very little about Marcy, who seemed never to generate gossip or stories of her own. Instead, she seemed content to know everyone else's gossip and live her life alone.

"Another toast!" Tracey called just as Marcy returned with their round. "To my beautiful, talented, and terribly kind half-sister, Elise. Where would any of us be without you?"

Elise bubbled with laughter, again so grateful for the family she'd discovered just in the nick of time. With another sip of Moscow Mule, she allowed herself to forget about her simmering curiosity about Marcy's life and instead fell into more conversation with her loved ones. Soon, they would scramble into the carriage with Kurt at the helm and dive into their warm beds at the cabin. In the morning, they would awaken to soft orange October light, the sizzle of bacon and eggs, and the allure of big mugs of morning coffee. How grateful she was for all of it.

Chapter Eight

That Wednesday afternoon, Elise donned her autumn jacket and a thick red hat and stepped into the swirling beauty of the day. Her wedding was only a week and a half away, and already, it seemed that everything had fallen into place. The wedding dress was fitted, the catering and flowers were finalized, the RSVPs were all accounted for, and the hotel rooms at the Grand Hotel had been reserved. Now, all Elise had to do was sit back and wait for time to pass. The wait was both blissful and nerve-racking, as it demanded only one question: *what could possibly go wrong?*

Wayne waited for Elise on the busted front porch of the abandoned house they'd purchased, his large hands over one of the only railings that seemed capable of holding him. "You'll never believe this, but we have a working stove!" he announced.

Elise walloped with laughter. "You're kidding." Wayne had met with a contractor the previous week to discuss how quickly they could get the house into working order. Their thought was if they could get the kitchen, one bathroom, and the bedroom sorted, they could then begin to spend more and more time at the house, building the world of their dreams there as they slowly shifted their lives out of Wayne's place. Sunday afternoon, after the bachelorette party had concluded, Elise and Wayne had selected a gorgeous stove for the kitchen, which the contractor had installed that day.

"The electrical system is in working order," Wayne said. "And he said that the plumbing is just fine as well. We just need to select a new tub, toilet, and sink for the downstairs and upstairs bathrooms."

Elise shrieked with excitement and leaped toward him, kissing him with her eyes closed. It was true what Cindy had said about building a new life with someone. You made up the new rules as you went along. Her and Wayne's rules, it seemed, buzzed with creativity and life.

"I thought that we could cook something here," Wayne said tenderly, his hands around her waist.

"And eat on the floor?" Elise cackled.

"You have no faith in me, do you?" Wayne grinned mischievously, took her hand, and led her into the creaking foyer. Once in the kitchen, he showed off the groceries that lined the counter, along with the foldable chairs and table, which he'd brought over from his place. On top of that, he'd brought a Bluetooth speaker, which he now turned on to play "At Last."

Elise wrinkled her nose, even as she swooned with happiness. "This is the cheesiest song you could have played."

"My lonely days are over," Wayne sang as he organized the ingredients for carbonara across the counter. "And life is like a song!"

Together, Elise and Wayne cooked the carbonara, sipped wine, and talked about their days. It was remarkable to think that this was the first time they would ever do this in their brand-new place, where they would certainly share dinner after dinner, both together and with family. There could only be one first time for anything. Elise wanted to cherish every moment.

Once at the foldable table, Elise and Wayne clinked wine glasses and began to eat, twirling the salty pasta through their forks and glancing up at once another excitedly, like teenagers in love. Midway through their meal, Elise heard herself say something that she'd been thinking for many months yet hadn't had the strength or the bravery to say aloud.

"I can't even begin to tell you how different this feels for me."

Wayne tilted his head. "What do you mean? Different?"

Elise set her fork to the side of her plate, suddenly overwhelmed with the immensity of what she wanted to say. "Sean... My ex."

Wayne nodded knowingly. Elise didn't speak of Sean often, as being cheated on and left after twenty years of marriage wasn't exactly an easy thing to talk about. Wayne understood that.

"It kind of felt like we had to get married, you know? Because of our babies. Because of the money that we didn't have. And because of societal expectation and all that," Elise continued. "That's not to say that my mother wanted us to get married. She did not!"

Wayne laughed appreciatively. "Yet again, I find myself very sad that I never got to meet your mother."

"She would have just loved you," Elise whispered sadly, her eyes cast down toward her pasta. How she missed her mother! How she wished she could be at this wedding, a wedding that Elise actually wanted! "I just mean to say that it's such a pleasure and a privilege to marry you. It's so different than my decision to marry Sean. When I look back at those last few weeks before my wedding to Sean, all I remember is fear and panic and stomach ache upon stomach ache."

"No stomach aches this week?" Wayne asked.

Elise shook her head. "Maybe if I eat too much pasta."

Wayne reached across the table and took her hand. His eyes glowed with love and understanding. Elise knew that Wayne couldn't say the same thing about Tara that she could about Sean and that a part of him would always love his first wife and miss her terribly. Elise had to understand that; she had to love that part of him, too.

After dinner, Elise and Wayne loaded up the dirty dishes so that they could wash them back at their working house, blew out the candles that Wayne had set up around the kitchen, and prepared to head back to the warmth of their first home. Before Wayne opened the door, however, Elise insisted upon heading upstairs to gather a stack of old diaries and albums from the trunk.

"Are you sure about that?" Wayne asked.

"I've been thinking about them all week," Elise explained as she rushed for the staircase, turning on the flashlight on her phone. "And aren't you curious about those blueprints? It's eerie, Wayne! We've discovered a secret!"

Wayne laughed as Elise snaked carefully up the staircase, then turned into the bedroom to drop down in front of the trunk. She then placed as many diaries and photo albums into her backpack as she could before she zipped it back up and retreated downstairs. The diaries and photo albums were terribly heavy, a metaphor for other people's memories.

Back at the house, Wayne passed out in a carbonara coma on the couch, which left Elise to sip tea in her robe and pore over the diaries and photo albums to her heart's content. Outside, the autumn winds shifted and tapped raindrops across the windowpanes. Elise's tea was warm and minty against her tongue. It calmed her mind as she began to read over long-lost diaries, the first of which was dated 1952— exactly seventy years ago.

The woman who'd written the 1952 diary was obsessive about details. She wrote of the lunches she'd packed her children (turkey and cheese, ham and cheese, watermelon), the temperature outside, the direction the wind was headed, and what the president had said on the radio. Never did she dare write about her emotions or her opinions, which was curious to Elise. For her, writing was all about emotion, about heart. *Why hadn't this woman allowed her writing to delve into that?* It was as though something had been lost.

Still, it was fascinating to read about the woman's life on the island seventy years ago. She discussed the fact that come August, she and the children would return to Lansing, where her husband worked as a banker.

"I will miss this beautiful house and its many secrets," the woman wrote in August 1952. Elise ached to know what these "secrets" might have alluded to, yet knew better than to expect anything more from the writer.

In fact, the writer hadn't even written her own name on the first page and only ever referred to herself as "I." This was perhaps the most curious thing of all.

Elise continued through the diaries, sometimes dipping in and out of people's handwriting, reading small stories from various decades, and trying to figure out how everyone was related to each other. The majority of the diaries were written by women, but a fair number of them had been written by men. The men spoke of hunting expeditions, fishing trips, their children (mostly discussing the boys they'd taken with them on hunting expeditions), and their jobs and money. Like the first woman's diary, the men hardly spoke of their own emotions. The weather was a frequent topic. Elise couldn't remember a single time she'd spoken of the weather in her diaries.

It was now a little past eleven at night. Wayne shifted on

the couch and eventually burst up, confused about where he was. "I'm going to bed," he said to Elise, rubbing his eyes. "Good night, my love. I hope you'll come to bed soon?"

Elise promised that she would, although she really wasn't so sure. She was now so deep in this other world, which seemed to be made up of families with the last names of Barry, Nederland, and Hamlet. The oldest diary was from the year 1913, while the last was scribed in the seventies. The seventies felt painfully close to the present until Elise reminded herself that the seventies had been a full fifty years ago. *How was that possible?*

Finally, Elise flipped over to the photo albums with the hope that she would be able to match faces with the names of the people in the diaries. Often, she was able to. There were several hunting photographs with fathers and sons in hunting clothing, a photo of a young boy with a very large fish that was labeled "Scott, 1966," and many photographs of birthday parties and picnics that seemed to feature many of the women mentioned in the diaries. It was remarkable to piece together the lives of these long-ago people and marvel that perhaps one of the only people who remembered all of them now existed in a retirement home outside of Los Angeles.

Outside, thunder rolled across Mackinac Island, and lightning flashed provocatively. Elise stood up from the table, suddenly realizing that she'd spent the better part of four hours trapped in other people's memories. Was she insane? Elise laughed to herself and wiped a Kleenex across her forehead, mopping up what seemed to be sweat. She'd really worked herself up over these stories.

Before she retreated to bed, Elise lifted one of the smaller photo albums from the table and flicked through it gently, eyeing the vintage colors of the photographs from the seventies and eighties. The clothing was remarkable: little dresses, bell-bottom jeans, and lace blouses. Elise's heart ached for this lost time.

One of the final few pages of the album featured several teenagers, all of whom glowed with youth and vitality. They stood upon sailboats, ate barbecue, and slowly aged through the pages, until they appeared in beards and womanly dresses, showing off their beauty in their twenties. The photographs were labeled 1984, 1985, and 1986, all years that Elise had lived back in Los Angeles.

Unfortunately, the photographs hadn't been labeled with anything but the years, as whoever had put the photo album together hadn't assumed that the names would be forgotten. Elise focused on the beautiful faces, trying to pair them with any people she had met during her time on the island.

One couple seemed to appear over and over again. They were particularly beautiful— the woman with soft blond-brunette hair and the man with sturdy sailor shoulders with jet-black hair. In one photograph, the man had his girlfriend lifted in his arms, and she tossed her head back, mid-laughter, as the Straits of Mackinac glittered around them. Love echoed off the page.

Suddenly, a stone dropped into the base of Elise's belly.

The woman in the man's arms wasn't just any woman.

That woman with the blond-brunette hair was none other than Marcy Plymouth, the owner and bartender of the Pink Pony.

Elise shivered with a sense of dread so powerful that she had to sit back down. For a very long time, as the thunder rolled across the hills outside, Elise studied the gorgeous face of Marcy, marveling at how hopeful her smile had been. *Who had the young man been?* Had Marcy once lived in the same house that Elise and Wayne had purchased? *Why, then, hadn't Marcy had some kind of say in the sale?*

Mysteries flung out before Elise, ones that intensified as

Elise remembered how often Tracey and Cindy had said that Marcy was "too pessimistic" for love. The Marcy in the photographs hadn't been too pessimistic about love. In fact, the Marcy in the photographs seemed to symbolize love and all its mysticisms.

What on earth had happened?

Chapter Nine

1987

"Are you sure you don't mind?" Marcy's voice rasped with stress as she twirled and twirled the phone cord around her finger. "Because I know how hard it's been for you, working both jobs."

"Don't worry about it, Marcy. I'm twenty-one years old. My body can take it," Kurt joked over the phone. "Just promise me I can have a big bucket of chicken wings in return, and we're in the clear."

Marcy laughed, her heart bursting. "Thank you. It's ridiculous, but I just don't have time to track him down. The bar is supposed to open in ten minutes, and..."

"Say no more, Marcy. I'm on my way," Kurt affirmed. "But you have to let me get off the phone first."

Marcy's giggles echoed from wall to wall in the little kitchen, even as the call cut out. She then burst toward the front window that looked out along Main Street, her eyes hungry for the first sight of Kurt as he scampered down the cobblestones. Sure enough, a split-second later, he appeared, still dressed in his captain's uniform from the ferry. The white of the uniform caught the bright July sunlight and flashed as he moved seamlessly through the crowd. Marcy waved out the window, her eyes closing slightly as she relaxed into the day.

Downstairs, Marcy began to stack beer bottles in the fridge as Kurt whipped a rag across each of the tables and chairs.

"No idea where the old man is?" Kurt asked, flipping his hair.

"I have a hunch, of course," Marcy said, heaving a sigh. "But let's put it this way. He's been drinking a lot lately."

"You'd think that a night at the police station would have cooled him down a bit," Kurt said.

"That's what Zane said," Marcy breathed, rubbing the top of her forehead with her palm. "Actually, he said a whole lot more than that. Gosh, Zane seems to dislike Dad more and more every day. Now that the Seattle job is in the bag, he acts like..."

But before Marcy could finish her thought, a loud rap came from the front door. There, several grinning tourists waved, hungry to enter to grab their first pints of the afternoon. Under his breath, Kurt whispered, "You'd think that they were raised in a barn."

"Just let them in," Marcy said. "Let's get this party started."

From the hours of three in the afternoon to one in the morning, Marcy and Kurt worked tirelessly— whipping through tables, pouring pints, mixing cocktails, laughing with guests, and generally keeping the Pink Pony at bay, even when it threatened to fall apart at the seams given its ever-increasing popularity. When Kurt finally flipped the OPEN sign to CLOSED, Marcy's knees buckled, and she nearly collapsed to the ground. Back in the kitchen, the chef on-hand hollered,

"Who wants to pour me a pint in return for a million chicken wings?"

"Sign me up for that," Kurt called back, limping behind the bar to pour them each a pint.

"Gosh. That was torture." Marcy dipped herself delicately against the edge of a barstool and stared at her shoes, which were black with gunk and cigarette ash.

Kurt placed her pint in front of her and urged her to drink it. "It'll help you calm down and get some sleep."

Marcy nodded and wrapped both hands around the beer, feeling woozy. Kurt disappeared into the kitchen to hand off the beer to the chef. Marcy then grabbed a package of peanuts from the countertop, tore it open, and ate one after another, slowly returning to consciousness. *How much money had the Pink Pony made that afternoon, evening, and late night? How much of the money would wind up in Marcy's hands? Knowing her father, it wouldn't be much.*

Ultimately, it didn't matter. Marcy knew that. When she was off in Seattle with Zane, she'd never work behind a bar again; there would always be money coming in. Already, she and Zane had decided to start their lives in a Seattle apartment, which would allow them time to search for the perfect home, one in which they would raise their children. She would dote on her children, make them little candies and cookies, and tell them creative stories that she made up on the spot.

Kurt returned to the bar to announce, "Benny says just another five minutes till the wings are ready."

"What a relief," Marcy said, trying on a smile. Through a yawn, she added, "I can't tell you how grateful I am for your help today, Kurt. Seriously. You're a—"

"A lifesaver. I know," Kurt teased.

Marcy stepped off the stool for a moment, giggling. "I'm going to run upstairs really quick." It had suddenly occurred to her that she probably looked like a mess, with black makeup running down her cheeks and sweat stains at her armpits. Something told her to go fix herself up, if only so that she could feel better again.

"Hurry back!" Kurt called as she scampered toward the back staircase.

When Marcy reached the back staircase, she was surprised to see that the door was wide open. Had she forgotten to close it when she'd run downstairs to open the bar for the day? Once she reached the top of the staircase, she found that the "official" entry door to the apartment was open, as well. Her heart jumped into her throat. Only when she stepped through the doorway could she fully reckon with the reality of the situation.

Someone had broken into the apartment and trashed it.

In the hallway, the lamp had fallen to the floor and lay crooked. The coatrack had fallen as well, tossing coats and jackets across the carpet. Marcy tip-toed into the kitchen to find food smeared across the countertops and the fridge wide open. "What the heck?" Slowly, Marcy continued her walk, finding bits and pieces of her house out of order until she reached her own room. There, it seemed, whoever had broken in had decided to really have a field day.

Marcy kept all her makeup and perfume things on a little desk in the corner. The perpetrator had essentially destroyed each glass bottle, casting perfume across the floor. The makeup utensils had been destroyed, and eyeshadow had snowed across the desk, the chair, and the carpeting. Many of her books had been torn from the shelves and tossed across the bed; several had pages taken out of them, and they fluttered across the rug forlornly.

As the tears thickened in her eyes, it was difficult for Marcy to fully make out the extent of the damage. When she stepped closer to the mirror at her makeup desk, however, she fully came to terms with the horror of it all.

There, written across the mirror in fat lipstick, were the words:

STAY AWAY FROM ZANE

Terrified, Marcy burst from the mirror and scampered down the hallway. A scream crawled out of her throat, but it wasn't loud enough to lift over the stereo system downstairs. Before long, she reached the telephone, where she dialed Zane's landline at the vacation house up near Pontiac Trail Head. As Zane had only just arrived back from Seattle the day before, he was still jet-lagged and had spent the majority of the day relaxing. It wasn't a surprise that he answered the phone with a chipper voice, knowing it could only be Marcy.

"I hope that's who I think it is."

Immediately, Marcy's breath calmed. "Oh my God, Zane. Oh my God."

"What's up, honey?" Zane's voice shifted. "Are you okay?"

Marcy explained what she could: that someone had broken into her apartment and destroyed a great deal of her stuff. For whatever reason, she decided to withhold the information about what this person had written in lipstick. It was too strange to report.

"Why don't I meet you outside the Pink Pony?" Zane suggested softly. "We can go for a walk. Calm down a little. After that, you can stay up here at my parents' place."

Marcy closed her eyes, considering this. On the one hand, she was terrified that her father would return home to find this mess. On the other, she was rather sure that he was already drunk and sleeping it off at one buddy's place or another. She could deal with the mess in the morning. Heck, maybe she would call the police. *That's what people did. Right?*

"Okay. Let's do it."

Downstairs, Kurt was already halfway through his bucket of chicken wings. His lips were dotted with barbecue sauce. As

Marcy whipped past him, he sensed something was amiss— but seemed to sense, too, that she didn't want to talk about it.

"Hey. I have to head out," she told him, slipping herself into her jean jacket. "Thank you again for helping out today. Make sure you take half the tips from the jar. And I'll get Daddy to write out your check this week. Gosh, you've worked just about one hundred hours this month, haven't you?"

Marcy spoke too quickly, revealing the panic in her voice. Kurt jumped off his stool, his eyebrows stitching together.

"Don't worry about a thing, Marcy," he said tenderly. "Just get some sleep tonight. Okay?"

Marcy nodded, her throat tightening. With a final wave, she leaped out into the blackness of the night and soon stumbled directly into Zane, who had marched down from his beautiful Victorian house on the hill to meet her. Once in his arms, she shook and shook against him, asking him to tell her that soon, it would all be all right again.

"We're going to start over, Marcy," Zane breathed, cupping her head with his hand as she cried.

"Sometimes, I feel like I just might suffocate if I stay here a moment longer," Marcy said, hiccupping. "But also, the thought of never being on Mackinac again terrifies me."

Zane's eyes echoed out infinite kindness. "I told you that we'll always have a link to Mackinac. We'll have a house here. A place that you can come to whenever you want to."

Marcy lifted her tear-filled eyes to meet his. Swaying slightly with the breeze off the Straits, she whispered, "How did I get so lucky?"

Zane's laughter echoed out across Main Street. "I ask myself the same thing every single day. Let's get back home, shall we? My jet lag is starting to lose its grip on me. I think I just might be able to sleep."

Chapter Ten

Present Day

The morning after Elise discovered the photographs of Marcy and this "handsome mystery man," Wayne left for the coffeeshop by five-thirty. He scribed a note, which he placed on the kitchen counter, that read: *"T-minus eight days till we say 'I do.' I'm the luckiest man in the world because I get to marry you."* Elise read it when she woke up around eight-thirty, bleary-eyed from her long night of scouring diaries and photo albums. Her heart stirred with a mix of longing and joy, grateful for the sort of man who left notes on countertops— even cheesy ones that rhymed.

Elise took it easy that morning, heading to yoga at a downtown studio, grabbing a cup of coffee at a jam-packed The Grind (where she hardly had time to say hello to Michael and didn't see Wayne at all), and taking a long, hot bath when she returned home. When she emerged from the tub, she had a text message from Tracey.

TRACEY: Cindy and I are thinking about making lunch for Dad up at the house. Want to join?

Elise texted back that she would love it.

ELISE: I stayed up a bit too late last night and probably won't get any writing done today. Lunch sounds grand.

The old Victorian home that Elise and Wayne had purchased sat heavy with shadows only six houses away from her father's. On her walk to Dean's, Elise took a moment in front of the house, her hands over the fence that lined the property as she again visualized both the past and the future of the old place. A funny part of her imagined Penny on the front stoop, a baby in her arms. Another imagined Brad, suntanned from his life in California, walking out the front door to wave hello. It was incredible what a house could do to your heart. It became so much more than its four walls.

Once at Dean's, Elise walked through the front door easily, no longer surprised at how welcomed she felt there. Tracey called, "Hello! We're in here!" from the kitchen, and Elise wandered through, sliding a hand over the dog Diesel's golden head.

"Hey there," Elise said, smiling at both Cindy and Tracey, who stood over the stove with mugs of tea. On the stove, a hearty lentil soup bubbled and spat.

"Hi!" Cindy and Tracey said in unison, hurrying over to hug Elise one at a time. Tracey then poured Elise some hot water and dropped a tea bag within as Diesel entered the kitchen happily and rolled into a ball in the corner.

"Where's Dad?" Elise asked.

"Here I am!" Dean marched down the hallway, his footfalls making the old house creak. He then came through the kitchen doorway, scraggly beard first, his cheeks ruddy from the chill. Elise had to guess that he'd already taken his brisk walk through the woods with his dog, the very thing that he attributed to his ever-present good health. "Good afternoon, darling Elise. How are you on this fine day?"

Elise laughed. "You're in a better mood than I am. Unfortunately, I didn't get much good sleep."

"That's terrible," Dean said, his eyes reflecting how much he meant it. "Let's see if your sisters and I can fix that bad mood of yours."

It wasn't so difficult for Elise to dig herself out from her early afternoon fatigue. Very soon, Tracey had her in stitches about something Emma had said about her pregnancy while Cindy discussed a recent dinner Ron had cooked for her that was "to die for." Dean spoke about his plans for snowmobiling this winter, a sport that Elise called "dangerous." The other Michiganders just laughed at her and said she was "too Californian to understand."

After lunch, Tracey and Cindy gathered the plates and insisted that Elise just hang out at the table and rest. Elise grimaced, but then thanked them. Dean remained at the table, his hand on Diesel's head as he lapped his tongue appreciatively.

After a strange moment of silence, Elise drummed up the nerve to ask her father a question that was heavy on her mind.

"Dad? How well do you know Marcy from the Pink Pony?"

Dean's fuzzy eyebrows lifted with surprise. "Marcy? Well, I suppose I've known Marcy since I got to Mackinac for the filming of *Somewhere in Time*, so around the same time that I met your mother. Back then, she was just a teenager, but already, that daddy of hers had her working behind the bar at the Pink Pony."

Elise's lips rounded with surprise. "Wow. I didn't know that her father had owned the place before her."

"Yes. Elliott Plymouth opened the place decades ago," Dean said. "I was never fond of him in the slightest. He was always shifting positions between being a drunken fool or mean as can be. I don't know how Marcy could stand it."

"Did he pass away?" Elise asked.

Dean clucked his tongue. Elise knew better than to expect her father to gossip.

"I had heard that he wasn't doing too well," Dean finally admitted. "But I can't say for certain where he is now. I suppose that I would have heard if he'd passed. Then again, Marcy has gotten so secretive over the years. She manages the bar, and that's all she wants anyone to know."

Elise nodded knowingly. "I've gotten the sense that she's difficult to get to know." After another pause, she finally admitted, "I've been going through these old diaries and photo albums that I discovered in the house down the road. It's been fascinating to pore through other people's memories."

"I suppose that's one of the reasons you didn't sleep well?" Dean teased.

"I felt like I couldn't stop," Elise admitted. "But toward the end of the very late night, I discovered several photographs of a young woman who seems like the spitting image of Marcy. In all of the photographs, she's with a very handsome young man with jet-black hair. They look like the quintessential American couple. And I couldn't help but wonder..."

Dean grimaced, his eyes on the ground. Elise understood, then. Dean detested that so many people on the island had gossiped about him and his affair with Elise's mother. In return, he'd done his best not to gossip about others.

Still, Elise ached to know.

"Everyone has always told me that Marcy hates romance. That she never wanted to settle down and have a family," Elise continued. "It was hard for me to believe. I mean, who hates love?"

"The only people who hate love are the ones who had it and lost it," Dean breathed.

Elise's heart leaped. This made a great deal of sense.

"Who was he?" Elise whispered.

Dean studied the ends of his perfectly clipped fingernails. "We were invited to the wedding," he began. "Mandy and I arrived early and sat on the bride's side, grateful to be invited to what many called 'the wedding of the summer.' Zane Hamlet and Marcy Plymouth were beloved across the island, perhaps because of what you said now. That they were the quintessential American couple. They made everyone remember what it was like to fall in love for the first time."

"Zane Hamlet," Elise breathed, remembering that one of the last names associated with the old Victorian she'd bought had been "Hamlet."

"But that afternoon of the wedding, we waited, and we waited," Dean continued. "Eventually, someone came to tell us that the wedding was off, that we should go home. Mandy and I left in a hurry, not wanting to get involved with the town gossip. Obviously, people latched onto that incident like their lives depended on it, probably making Marcy's life a living hell for a little while. Pity can destroy a person. But what was Marcy supposed to do after that? She never went to college. All she had was the Pink Pony. She stayed here on the island, eventually taking over the Pink Pony for herself when Elliott retired. That's all I know, unfortunately."

"And you never figured out why he left?" Elise asked, heartbroken over the story of Marcy's young and broken love.

"No. People speculated right and left, but I never knew what was true and what wasn't," Dean continued. "I've told you the basic facts that I know from my perspective. That's all I can really do."

A little while later, Elise returned to the kitchen to find that her sisters had finished with the dishes and were about to plate some hot apple pie with ice cream. Elise dropped her head back and groaned. "You live better on this island than anywhere else, I swear. Before I came here, I hadn't had ice cream for years, let alone pie."

"Someone needs to go out to California and show people how to live," Tracey joked.

"Ha. You should become a dessert missionary," Elise said, crossing her arms distractedly. As her sisters continued to jabber, Elise's own heart and mind turned toward Marcy, who seemed mostly alone in the world, having built walls around herself to keep everyone out. Cindy, Tracey, and the rest of the island considered her "cold-hearted" or, at least, too practical for love. Elise wasn't so sure. To her, everyone needed love. It was like oxygen.

Chapter Eleven

That Saturday, Marcy performed the basic rituals of a typical morning. She awoke at five, went for a six-mile run, showered, ate a simple yet nutritional breakfast, took inventory, called her father's nursing home for an update (he was "just the same as he'd been two days ago," when Marcy had visited), and prepared herself for a very busy afternoon and evening at the Pink Pony. Life as she knew it had entered a sort of dreamlike state, which allowed her to perform each action for the millionth time without thinking about it. She was fifty-six years old, but she could have been any age. Someday, maybe, she would give up her life at the bar and head somewhere new. Maybe at sixty-two or sixty-five or seventy-three.

Kurt stopped by around noon for a grilled cheese sandwich with ham and a light beer. He was chipper and friendly, talking about a recent book he'd read about Roman history, which Marcy was grateful to hear about, if only because it sounded more important than the typical drivel people told her about at the bar. Kurt always seemed hungry for knowledge, a fact that often made Marcy confused as to why he never ran off and studied something at a university.

By twelve-thirty, a steady stream of customers arrived at the bar for lunch and drinks. Marcy flung into action, taking orders and typing them into the brand-new computer she'd purchased, one that hardly seemed related to the old cash register she and her father had used back in the eighties and nineties. It was remarkable what technology could do for your business. At least, that's what all these new-fangled computer companies wanted you to think.

When Marcy was busy taking a round of orders at a table of ten, her cell phone began to blare on the countertop. Annoyed, Marcy turned quickly and said to Kurt, "Can you answer that really quickly? I'm expecting a call from the guy who delivers the beer."

Kurt snapped his fingers and said, "I'm on it." He then hustled around the counter and grabbed her cell. "Good afternoon. This is Marcy Plymouth's phone."

By then, Marcy had already turned back to continue to take orders from the ten people before her, most of whom seemed unwilling or unable to read the menu correctly. Marcy patiently listed the condiments that always came on the burger. Just as she'd reached "mustard and pickle," a hand came over her shoulder.

"Marcy? Can I speak with you for a moment?" Kurt's voice was stricken.

Marcy turned around, eyes widening. She didn't even bother to tell the table she'd be right back. Probably, they would write a bad review of the experience on Google. Right then, Marcy couldn't care less.

In the back hallway, Marcy pressed her phone against her ear and listened as the same woman she'd just spoken to at her father's nursing home explained that Elliott Plymouth had suffered a stroke early that afternoon and had been rushed to the Cheboygen hospital.

Marcy stuttered with shock. "I just called you. I just asked you how he was." She wasn't sure why she wanted to pin the blame on this poor woman. The blame had to go somewhere, she supposed.

In a flash, Marcy called the young woman who sometimes picked up shifts at the Pink Pony and asked her to come in "as soon as possible." When she arrived, Marcy and Kurt bundled up in coats, scarves, and hats and raced to Kurt's boat, which transported them quickly across the Straits. Marcy wasn't sure why she hadn't questioned why Kurt was right there with her. It just seemed natural that he would tag along.

When they reached Marcy's clunky car at the garage, Kurt ordered her to sit in the passenger seat.

"You're shaking, Marcy," Kurt pointed out softly. "Just let me take over."

Marcy was disgruntled, agitated at the idea that she couldn't handle the simple task of driving to her father's side. Still, she slid the keys into Kurt's hands and buckled herself into the passenger side.

By the time they got to the hospital, Marcy's father had been stabilized. The doctor reported that it was a minor stroke, one that would require a bit of rehabilitation. "He should be able to return to his relatively normal life within a month or two," he explained. "We'll keep him here at the hospital overnight to make sure he's all right, and then, we'll return him to the nursing home tomorrow. Of course, you're welcome to go see him, although he's currently sleeping."

Marcy stood at her father's side for the better part of twenty minutes. Shock rolled through her. There he was, the man she'd loved her entire life— for better or for worse. His skin was terribly pale; his lips were chapped. His hands looked weak, limp, and overly large, as though he'd never used them for anything at all. Marcy realized that she'd expected to lose her father that day. Tears welled in her eyes and drifted down her cheeks. What would happen when she lost the old man for good? She would be alone in the world. She wouldn't have anyone left to love.

Back in the lobby, Kurt jumped to his feet and gave her a warm smile. "I can't imagine that you've bothered to eat anything since breakfast," he said.

It was true. Marcy wavered as she walked along Kurt all the way back to the car. Once there, she nodded in agreement to his suggestion that they eat at a Mexican restaurant just down the road.

"It's been ages since I had a good chimichanga," Kurt reported as he drove the car from the hospital lot.

It was surreal to sit in a restaurant that wasn't the Pink Pony. Around their table, unfamiliar families and couples ate and laughed together, crunching on tortilla chips and shrieking at the spices in their burritos. Marcy ordered a cheese and onion quesadilla with black beans, while Kurt ordered a chimichanga with beef. Both decided on margaritas with a thick line of salt around the rim.

Marcy drank her first margarita a little too quickly and closed her eyes against the wave of sorrow that came over her. "Gosh, Kurt. I can't thank you enough for driving me out here today."

Kurt's voice was soft. "You know that you don't have to thank me for anything. I'm here for you."

Marcy nodded, her chin quivering. "You've always been there for me. Through everything. Gosh, I can't even begin to thank you for all of it."

What was she doing? She never got this sappy. But how could she pull herself together? She'd nearly lost her father. Here she sat with Kurt, her only friend in the world. How had her life gotten so dark?

"I just hope that I've been there enough for you over the years," Marcy breathed, forcing her eyes open. She sipped the last of her margarita and managed to add, "I know it was hard when things didn't work out with Stephanie."

Kurt's eyes dropped to the basket of chips between them. They hardly ever spoke about Stephanie, Kurt's first and only wife. They'd married after a very brief courtship but had divorced after a little less than two years. At the time, Kurt and Marcy had been in their late twenties, still with plenty of years left to love and lose. Now, at fifty-six, Marcy wasn't so sure.

"It happens," Kurt said with a soft shrug. "Marriage is a fifty-fifty game these days."

"I never even made it down the aisle," Marcy reminded him.

"I'll never forgive that bastard," Kurt said, his voice resolute.

Marcy swallowed the lump in her throat, trying to shove away the dark memories. More than anything, she wanted another margarita.

"Stephanie always accused me of caring more about the Pink Pony than about our marriage," Kurt said suddenly.

Marcy's eyes flicked back toward his. He'd never told her that.

"I mean, I understood that you needed me down there at the bar," Kurt continued rapidly. "Elliott never hired enough people, and he always managed to slip out right when it got too busy for you to handle it by yourself."

"Again, I've always been so grateful," Marcy muttered.

"It's fine. I enjoy that work," Kurt said with a wave of his hand. "It's just that Stephanie didn't exactly appreciate it when I ran out on her every night around the same time. When she suggested that I cared more about the Pink Pony than our marriage, I realized that— well, maybe she was right."

Marcy laughed quietly, overwhelmed. Her eyes again dropped to the chips. "That's ridiculous. It's just an old bar."

"Yeah," Kurt said quietly, clearly unsure of how to proceed.

Kurt and Marcy sat in silence for what felt like an impossibly long minute. Marcy blinked several times, at a loss. All of their dramatic stories now seemed so long ago. Probably, everyone around them at the Mexican restaurant thought they were a married couple, one who had no idea what to say to one another anymore.

Finally, Marcy breathed, "I'm going to stay the night at the hospital. That way, I can make sure Dad's comfortable at the nursing home tomorrow."

Kurt nodded. "I can get us a couple of hotel rooms for the night."

But Marcy shook her head. "No. I need you to go back and check on the Pink Pony. There's no telling how many days I'll need to stay out here, and I can't keep the place closed for too long. I rely on that money for Dad's nursing home bills."

Kurt's face was stony. Marcy could hardly look at it. After another pause, he sipped the rest of his margarita and crunched on a chip.

"I can come back and pick you up when you're ready," he tried.

"Don't worry. I'll figure out a way back," Marcy affirmed, her voice stiffening.

As they continued to eat in silence, a voice at the very bottom of Marcy's soul screamed out. *Why did she push everyone away from her? Why couldn't she let anyone in?* Kurt was her best friend in the world— and even now, as he showed her the depths of his love for her, she pushed him out. She was doomed to walk the earth alone. It was crystal clear, even now.

Chapter Twelve

The phone call that Elise received that Sunday morning at nine was not a happy one.

"Elise? You're not going to like what I'm about to say."

"Hit me, Peter. I can handle it," Elise said, scrunching her nose at the film editor's voice. By her count, the film editor was still awake at six a.m. Los Angeles time, probably after spending all of the previous afternoon and night editing the film that she, Malcolm, Tracey, and a number of other talented artists had put together that summer. If Peter had bad news for her, she had to take it— even six days before her wedding. The film was important to her. It was her responsibility to make it right.

That morning, Wayne and Michael were hard at work at The Grind. As Elise walked through the front door, she marveled at the swarm of tourists and locals alike, all of whom lined up at the coffeeshop counter, their lips dripping with hunger for freshly baked croissants, chocolate-glazed donuts, little apple and pumpkin tarts, plus cappuccinos, lattes, and Americanos.

"Yo! Aunt Elise!" Michael waved from behind the register, flashing his familiar and mischievous grin. "Wayne's in back."

Elise dove through the hive of hungry coffeeshop dwellers and swung through the door, headed for Wayne's office. Once she reached it, she fell against the doorframe and studied his profile, there as he bent toward the computer and muttered something to himself.

"Howdy, stranger," she teased, her heart lifting.

Wayne bucked around, eyes nearly popping from his head. It was clear that he and Michael had had a very frantic morning, one that would leave both of them in heavy naps by five p.m. that evening. By then, Elise would already be off the island, headed west. How could she break it to him?

Elise kissed Wayne tenderly, her eyes closed. He wrapped his hands around her waist and lifted her onto his desk, his eyes alight with curiosity. "To what do I owe the pleasure?"

Elise explained the situation as best as she could, her anxiety growing. Back when she'd been married to Sean, a conversation like this might have made him fly off the handle. (Again, she considered the fact that her love for her career had pushed Sean toward his mistress. This wasn't a healthy thought to have, which she knew all too well. Still, it was always there, lurking in the back of her mind.)

"So, you'll head out to LA for a few days, tie up loose ends, and meet me at the altar on Saturday?" Wayne said simply, as though he spoke about the weather.

Elise blinked, surprised. "You're really cool about me flying across the continent six days before our wedding?"

Wayne shrugged. "I don't want the film to affect Friday, Saturday, or the next few weeks after that. After the wedding, it's just you, me, and the Bahamas, baby."

Elise dropped her head back, shivering with laughter.

Wayne tilted his head knowingly and added, "And I'd guess that you'd want to say a final goodbye to that city. It's where you grew up. It's where your mother is buried. And it's where Brad still lives. The film is important; I know that. But the other stuff is just as important, perhaps more so."

Elise leaped forward, her arms around Wayne's sturdy shoulders as she exhaled all the air from her lungs. "You get it," she whispered. "You really do."

Not long after, Tracey appeared at The Grind to say good-bye. Her eyes were rimmed pink, and her cheeks seemed oddly hollow from stress. She sat across from Elise at the table in the corner and adjusted a large bag against her ankle.

"It sounds awfully stressful to fly out at a moment's notice," Tracey said.

Elise waved a hand. "You know the business at this point. Besides, I understood that this sort of thing could happen when I moved out to Mackinac. I'm a screenwriter living outside of Los Angeles. Am I insane?"

Tracey laughed knowingly and adjusted a curl behind her ear. "I'm glad you told me before you left. I have a few things that I was hoping you could fly out to LA for me?"

Elise's lips parted with surprise. She hadn't expected this.

"That's only if you have space in your suitcase," Tracey continued, stuttering. "If you don't, I totally understand. I can mail them."

"What do you have?" Elise asked softly.

Tracey ruffled through the bag on the floor, removing two beautiful child-sized dresses from her boutique, along with a book that Elise didn't recognize. Tracey's cheeks burned red with shame as she explained, "Malcolm's daughter looks so adorable in the little dresses he picked out at the boutique over the summer. I wanted to make sure she has a few new ones for autumn." Tracey paused for a moment, then added, "And I told Malcolm all about this writer. He was interested in reading this book, or at least, he said that he was interested. Maybe that was just a lie to make me feel better."

"That's silly!" Elise cried, her heart cracking at the edges. "Malcolm will love these gifts."

"It isn't stupid to send them along with you?" Tracey asked. "I get in my head about our relationship over the summer. Maybe it meant nothing to him. Maybe it was just a silly summer fling."

Elise wrapped her hand around Tracey's on the table, over-whelmed with emotion. How could she explain to her half-sister that she was really so worthy of love? But before she could, Tracey just shook her head and insisted, "You should head out. I know that you have a very long trip ahead of you." She stood abruptly, adjusting her skirt as she added, "There are a few snacks in the bag for you as well. Emma is crazy for baking right now."

Elise stood, her eyes welling with tears as she hugged Tracey close. "She's nesting," Elise suggested of Emma, thinking of the pregnancy and all there was to look forward to. She met Tracey's gaze and said, "I'll tell Malcolm you said hello. And I'll give him the presents. Okay?"

Tracey sniffed and turned herself away. "Thank you."

The following several hours weren't easy. Elise kissed Wayne goodbye, grabbed her suitcase, and headed to the ferry, where she watched the rock she called home fade into the shimmering Straits of Mackinac. Once on Mackinaw City soil, she grabbed her car from the garage and began the long drive down to Detroit. Her flight would leave at five-thirty-five that evening, and during the flight, she would watch the edits of the film, make notes, and come to terms with the enormous amount of work that she, the film editor, and Malcolm would have to do that week. If all went well, she would fly back to Detroit by Thursday, drive back to Mackinac, and prepare to marry the love of her life. This was the life of showbiz, she knew. This was the life that, God willing, she would live the rest of her days.

Chapter Thirteen

Elise rented a beautiful apartment in downtown Beverly Hills for the week ahead. When she arrived in LA, she slipped back into the heat of the air as though it was a warm sweater. The palm trees fluttered in the light breeze, and a gooey pink sunset spread out across the sky, a reminder of how far she'd traveled and how, if you traveled far enough away, you could slip easily into another life.

That night as she settled between the thousand-count sheets of her rental apartment bed, she texted her son with news of her arrival.

ELISE: Hey, buddy. I'm in the city this week. Would love to see you if you're not too busy.

Brad, who was never too far away from his phone, texted a few minutes later.

BRAD: What! That's incredible. It's your final week of being "single." Let's celebrate!

Elise laughed, exhaustion pouring over her as she typed back.

ELISE: You'll have to teach me how to be cool in

this city again. I think I've lost all track of what that means.

Elise settled into a deep sleep, eventually bursting awake at the first ring of her alarm clock at six the following morning. By seven, she was hard at work in the editing room with both Peter and Malcolm, immersed in the world that she'd created. During those hours, she no longer felt like "Elise, Wayne's fiancé." Rather, she felt like an artist, a writer, and a creative person, someone who existed wholly to make stories that reflected the human experience. She was grateful that she could be both at once.

At two that afternoon, Malcolm announced that he was starving and suggested that they head out for lunch.

"I don't know," Elise said, her nostrils flared. "We should get through the rest of this section before we take a break."

But Malcolm wouldn't hear of it. "We can't drive ourselves crazy," he said. "Let's sit down with some burritos and discuss what's next. We have to work smarter than this, and smart, in my world, means eating well."

Elise knew that Malcolm was right. Ten minutes later, she, Malcolm, and Peter sat around a little table at a local burrito place, no longer thinking of work. Peter told a funny story about his toddler, who seemed like a terror, while Malcolm described his advancements in sign language, which was required for his daughter.

"It's hard enough to be a good parent," Elise said, her eyes widening. "Let alone having to learn a whole new language to be able to communicate with them!"

Malcolm nodded evenly. Before he could respond, Elise snapped her fingers and said, "I just remembered. I have a gift for you back at the office."

Malcolm's eyes glittered. "What kind of gift? Aren't you the one getting married? I should be the one giving gifts to you."

Elise waved a hand. "This is something else."

Malcolm dropped his gaze to the beef burrito between his palms. Peter glanced at Elise, then back at Malcolm, clearly confused. After another pause, Malcolm muttered, "I hope she's okay?"

Obviously, he'd figured out that the gifts were from Tracey. Malcolm was no dummy.

"She's just fine. Over the moon about her coming grand baby," Elise continued softly.

"I imagine she sent along something for my daughter," Malcolm affirmed.

"Dresses," Elise said. "And a book for you. Something she said that she thought you'd really like."

"I'm sure I will. Tracey has exceptional taste," Malcolm said.

Elise's lips parted with surprise. If she wasn't mistaken, Malcolm spoke of Tracey with an air of sorrow, as though he mourned something that he could never fully have. Yet again, Elise thought of Marcy and this mystery man, Zane Hamlet. Why had he left her at the altar like that? *In each photograph, Zane and Marcy's love had sizzled with expectation. What did it mean that Malcolm and Tracey loved one another? What did it mean that Zane and Marcy had once loved one another? Did any of that loss add up to anything?*

That evening, Elise returned to her Beverly Hills apartment at around six-thirty. There, she changed into a pair of sweatpants and a sweatshirt and hovered over a bag of chips as she snacked, feeling stressed from the day. A few minutes later, the doorbell rang. When she opened it, Elise was surprised and very pleased to find her only son, Brad, there in a pair of jeans and a t-shirt, his hands shoved in his pockets. She flung forward and wrapped her arms around him, overwhelmed by his handsome portrait. Yet again, she was reminded that he looked so much like Dean had "back in the day." This resemblance had been one of the ways that Elise had figured out that she was actually Dean Swartz's daughter.

"You didn't message me back!" Brad protested as he entered. "I kept asking if you could meet tonight."

Elise scrunched her nose. "I'm so sorry, hon. I'm a bit of a stress ball."

Brad laughed. "I know how you get when you're in the middle of a movie." He dropped easily onto the couch in the living room and glanced around, clearly impressed. For the first time, Elise acknowledged a glint of sadness in his eyes, something that she hadn't viewed in him in any of their meetings over the summer.

"Do you want to grab something to eat?" Elise asked her son, lifting her eyebrow.

"Oh. Yes, please. Very much."

Elise smiled knowingly and tilted her head toward the front door. "Why don't we head out? There are tons of good places around here."

"Don't I know it," Brad said mischievously, slowly becoming himself again. "I'm the one who lives in Los Angeles, Mom. Not you."

"Wow. Someone is throwing shade," Elise teased.

"Mom, nobody says 'throwing shade' anymore," Brad said. "Get with the times. Okay?"

Elise laughed, scampering toward her bedroom to change into something fancier for the night ahead. Brad was right; this was her final week of being "single." She was grateful to find small moments to enjoy herself— and get to the bottom of whatever it was that made Brad look so sorrowful.

Brad suggested dim sum, a brand-new place that "everyone was raving about" that just happened to have a location a few blocks away from Elise's apartment. It was a welcome surprise to be able to walk anywhere in Los Angeles, where Elise had spent the better part of her life trapped in traffic. Together,

Elise and Brad walked easily, their shoulders back as they chatted about the Los Angeles Dodgers, Brad's new job, and "how scary it was" to be twenty-two.

"There are all these paths in life," Brad said contemplatively, palming the back of his neck. "I just worry that I'll choose the wrong one."

Elise was surprised at how easily Brad spoke to her, his eyes toward the horizon. Before she could properly respond, however, they reached the dim sum restaurant, and Brad was in conversation with the host, who seated them at a corner table outside without waiting. Very soon after they were seated, a line formed around the block, with diners eyeing their table jealously. Elise beamed at Brad, grateful that her son could show her the best of the best in Los Angeles, which was something she'd so often done for her own mother.

After they ordered, Elise stepped tentatively back toward the conversation Brad had begun about "life paths." Perhaps this had something to do with the sorrow that continued to beam out from his eyes. This time, Brad casually side-stepped the questions, sipping his beer. He then said, "Why don't you tell me about this new house you and Wayne bought?" Elise blushed, sensing that he didn't want to tell his mother what was really on his mind. That would have to be okay.

Elise talked about the house, about their plans for the kitchen and the dining area, and about the bedrooms that she "couldn't wait" to have Brad and Penny stay in.

"My dream is that you and Penny will spend summers out on Mackinac with Wayne and I," Elise said wistfully, knitting her brows together. "Wayne could teach us all how to sail, and we could spend our evenings around a bonfire, cooking s'mores."

Brad laughed. "You're such a dreamer, Mom."

"Give me one reason that I shouldn't be!" Elise returned, teasing him.

Brad took another sip of beer, eyeing the passing tourists and locals alike, most of whom seemed incredibly fashionable and very into themselves. This was the Los Angeles way.

"I guess I have no reason not to spend time on Mackinac," Brad said finally, his voice cracking slightly. "There's nothing for me here right now."

"Come on," Elise said, her eyes widening. "You're Mr. Los Angeles. Here we are, at the restaurant that you picked out yourself because it's the 'new, hip spot.'"

Brad shrugged and folded his hands across the table. "There's always a new, hip spot. There will be a new one next week and the one after that. Right now, I feel so tired of this non-stop movement toward something better. I wonder what we're losing when we're always searching for what we don't have."

Elise's lips parted with surprise. She'd always known that her son was intelligent and soft-hearted— but this was something else, something that spoke of an inner life that she hadn't assumed he had. She'd been incorrect.

"It sounds like you're thinking about your priorities," Elise breathed, grateful that he'd returned to the topic of "life paths."

Brad shifted uneasily on his chair. "I almost feel like the universe brought you here this week for my sake. Not that I believe in things like 'the universe' or whatever. But..." Here, he dropped his gaze to the table. "I feel very lonely this week. I hate to admit it, but I needed my mother. And now, here you are."

Elise's eyes welled with tears, which she hurriedly blinked back. She wouldn't ruin the moment by blubbering about her love for her son. "Honey, what happened?"

"Eh. A breakup." Brad tore the tongs of his fork through his dim sum. "People go through them all the time, you know? I know that it doesn't make me special. But I really thought that we had a future together, she and I."

Elise had met Brad's girlfriend numerous times and had, admittedly, always assumed that the two would get married. She prayed that her disappointment didn't play out across her face. The last thing Brad needed was Elise's own thoughts on the matter. She placed her hand over Brad's on the table and whispered, "I'm so sorry, Brad. Breakups never get any easier. And no matter what anyone says, they're not normal, either. It's like a small death of something."

Brad's face was stony. "Yeah. For all these years, I thought that we would get married. That was my life plan. But now, it's like every opportunity is in front of me, but all I want to do is crawl into bed and sleep."

Elise remembered the months after her own separation and divorce, during which she'd had to live with the truth that her husband had cheated on her. During that time, she'd spent a great deal of time sick in bed, watching the shadows as they played out across the wall. To her, her life had been really and truly over.

How silly to think now that, really, her life had only just begun.

She knew she couldn't tell Brad that the breakup would allow him to find "something better" and "learn something more about himself." Words like that never really helped.

"It's funny because we both kind of said it at the same time," Brad breathed, his eyes on the steaming dim sum. "The air had shifted between us. We no longer held hands or touched each other or..." He trailed off, clearly uninterested in explaining the details of his love life to his mother. "And one day, we just looked at each other and admitted that we were better off as friends."

Elise's eyes became slits. "And have you stayed friends since the breakup?"

"It just happened two weeks ago," Brad admitted. "We've hardly spoken. I sent her a few text messages, and she only responded to a few. I think the thing is, we were both pretty done with the relationship. But now that it's over, we realize the extent of what we lost. Messy, huh?"

"Messy," Elise affirmed. She then dropped her chin to her chest to add, "I hope you know that you can come out to Mackinac any time you want to. You can regroup there. Think about what's next."

Brad lifted his shoulder. "I might take you up on that. Someday."

Elise tried a smile. "The winter is a lot cozier than it seems. We could drink hot toddies, paint pictures."

But Brad just shook his head. "I have to figure this out on my own right now, Mom. But thank you."

Elise knew better than to push the issue. Instead, she made it her mission to spend as much time with her son that week as possible— to buy him dinners, laugh with him, and recount old stories from the past. He'd given her an incredible gift in telling her that he'd needed her; here she was, ready to give him all the love in the world. One day soon, this pain would be a wretched memory, one with pockets of sunshine and plenty of dim sum.

Later that night, as Brad slept in the other room of the apartment Elise had rented that week, Elise paced, too overwhelmed from the long flight, the hard workday, and the conversation with Brad to sleep. Her thoughts spun with memories of her life with Sean, fear of her upcoming life with Wayne, fear for her babies' futures, and, of course, images of Zane and Marcy, who'd taken up permanent residence in her mind.

As a writer, she was accustomed to making connections between stories and hunting for metaphors. She couldn't help but see the beauty and pain of learning about Zane and Marcy's doomed engagement mere days before her own marriage to Wayne. How strange that she and Wayne had purchased the very house that Zane's family had once owned for generations. Obviously, that house was filled with ghosts for Marcy.

Dean had told Elise that Zane Hamlet was an architect, someone who was expected to be "something," something bigger than the island could have allowed. This explained why nobody had ever returned to the old Victorian home, why they'd allowed generations of memories to die out in that house. This also probably explained the old blueprints of the long-forgotten house. *Had Zane wanted to build that as his and Marcy's summertime home?* She shivered at the number of hours Zane had assuredly put into drawing the plans. *How had someone so in love fallen out of it so quickly? What did any of it mean?*

The clock on the wall in the bedroom read 2:14 a.m. Elise rolled her eyes, annoyed with herself and her anxious mind. Slowly, she shifted herself beneath the sheets of the cloud-like bed, then propped her laptop on her lap. There would be no sleep until she learned something about Zane Hamlet. *Plus, hadn't Alex said that the person they'd purchased the old house from now lived in a nursing home somewhere outside of Los Angeles? Did that mean that Zane lived in the city somewhere?*

With purposeful fingers, Elise typed: **Zane Hamlet Architect.**

Elise was gobsmacked at the number of results. Page after page spoke about Zane Hamlet's "prosperous architectural designs," his "big strides to make the architecture world more female-friendly," and his multiple projects, both in the United States and abroad. Elise clicked through the "images" and discovered that this Zane Hamlet was, indeed, the very man in the photos with Marcy— somewhere in his mid-fifties, with salt and pepper hair, broad shoulders, and that same handsome smile. It didn't take long for Elise to learn that Zane had married his wife, Bethany, in 1992 and gone on to have four children. On his website, there was a single photograph of Zane and his family, where they stood in front of a massive Sequoia tree, Zane and Bethany in the back and their four children in front of them. Beneath the photograph, in a simple paragraph, Zane called himself a "family man, first and foremost."

Elise's eyes bugged out. She felt as though she peered into the life that Marcy had expected for herself. Those children should have been Marcy's children. That vacation to Sequoia National Park should have been Marcy's vacation. *Why, then, was Marcy still hard at work behind the bar of the Pink Pony? What had happened?*

Elise couldn't help it; she burned with curiosity.

After a few more clicks through his website, Elise was pleased and unsurprised to learn that Zane Hamlet had been the very architect to design the multi-million-dollar mansion that belonged to her friend and ex-colleague, a producer named Benny, who lived in Malibu. Elise hadn't seen Benny in over five years, but the two had always gotten along well.

Sometime before 3:30 that morning, Elise scribed an email to Benny.

Hey, Benny!

Long time no see. I hope you've been well. I've kept track of your projects over the past few years (I absolutely ADORED The Brothers' Walk) *and have been unsurprised to watch your talents blossom.*

Question: I'm in the beginning stages of hiring an architect to build myself and my fiancé a new place. As I always adored your home (simply gorgeous!), I thought I'd reach out to you for Zane Hamlet's personal contact information.

All the best to you,

Elise Darby

Chapter Fourteen

Marcy still hadn't made it back to Mackinac. She'd rented a hotel room in Cheboygen, no more than a fifteen minute walk from her father's nursing home, where she spent the majority of her days. Since the stroke, her father was listless and gray-faced. He still hadn't mustered the strength to speak, although the doctors informed her that very soon, they expected that Elliott would begin to try out syllables again.

It was the Tuesday after the stroke, and Marcy sat outside the physical therapy office, watching as the physical therapist spoke gently to her father, as though he were a child. Elliott's eyes looked somewhere past the physical therapist's shoulders, pinned to the back wall. Marcy had the sudden instinct to tell the physical therapist about the time after Marcy's mother had died when Elliott's rage and sorrow had been like a physical monster in the space they'd shared together. Once, he'd thrown a lamp across the room, where it had shattered against the far wall, casting its shards in all corners. Marcy had discovered pieces of the lamp beneath the couch even years later, sights that had immediately brought her back to the horrors of that time.

"It's going to be a long road," the physical therapist said, her eyes bright. "But Elliott's a strong guy. He's going to get through this. Aren't you, Elliott?" She wheeled his chair out from the physical therapy office and passed it over to Marcy, who thanked her with a crackling voice. "I hope you're hanging in there, okay?" the therapist asked Marcy, although Marcy knew there was no real answer to that. In the physical therapist's line of work, people had strokes all the time. Probably, she dealt with women like Marcy all the time— women left to pick up the pieces of the end of someone's life. What made Marcy different, she supposed, was that Elliott was the only person left in her life to love.

That afternoon, Marcy sat on the couch in her father's suite and stared at the glowing television, which again produced the game show that her father particularly liked. A part of her prayed silently that Elliott would suddenly explode with the answers to the questions on screen before berating each of the contestants for being, in his words, "raging idiots." Instead, Elliott continued to stare straight ahead, his lips partly open. His eyes caught the rectangle light of the television. It was difficult to say if he registered any of it in the slightest.

Since "the incident" with Kurt the previous week, Marcy and Kurt hadn't spoken on the phone at all. Instead, Kurt texted her with updates from the bar, ensuring that she knew that he "had it handled." Marcy recognized that she'd accidentally destroyed something between them; maybe they couldn't rebuild it.

But then again, if Kurt actually nursed some idea about a romance between them— wasn't it better that he understood she wasn't interested? She'd had her chance at love, at family. She was now fifty-six years old and far too old to become anything but what she was.

Still, it pained her to hear that Kurt's ex, Stephanie, had partially left him because of Kurt's apparent allegiance to Marcy. Marcy had always thought the world of Kurt; she'd wanted him to become something bigger and better than his roots. What had begun as a summer's job at Shepler's Mackinac Island Ferry had turned into a lifelong commitment. He'd never officially hung up that captain's hat. As far as she knew, he'd never even made it down to Florida for vacation, let alone for all those jobs he'd once dreamed of.

"Do you have any regrets, Dad?" Marcy suddenly asked her father, who couldn't even grunt with an answer.

On television, the game show switched over to a commercial break for organic dog food. Marcy lifted her fingers and rubbed her eyes, upon which she hadn't put on even the slightest hint of makeup since arriving to Cheboygen. When she slipped into the bathroom, the mirror gave her an image of an overly tired woman with big bags beneath her eyes and stringy hair.

In the bathroom, Marcy washed her face and her hands and tied up her hair into a bun. For not the first time, she remembered how, back when she'd been twenty-one and preparing to marry Zane, she'd allowed him to stand in the doorway of the bathroom as she'd brushed her teeth and washed her face. *Had that level of intimacy scared him off?* She'd thought that they'd been inseparable, so intimate that he could see her without makeup or with toothpaste suds on her lips and think nothing of it. When she'd awoken at his family's place, her hair had looked like a chaotic mop, and he'd cackled and tried to style it every which way. At the time, Marcy had thought, *I've found the funniest man in America. How did I get so lucky?*

In the next room, Elliott coughed twice. The sound terrified Marcy, as she hadn't heard him make a single noise since the stroke. She hustled into the next room and watched as the side of his face that could still move settled back into place.

"You okay, Dad?" Marcy asked.

Of course, her father didn't answer.

Marcy settled back on the couch and crossed her ankles, trying to shove away the aching loneliness that had taken up permanent residency in her belly. Again, she tried to tell herself that everything that had ever happened had been for the best. After all, if she'd actually gone to Seattle with Zane all those years ago, would Elliott have been alone in a room like this, listless and waiting to die? *Would anyone have gotten him a spot in the nursing home in the first place?*

Again, Marcy remembered the old expression that her father had so often used when she was younger. "It is what it is." Every time he'd said it, Marcy had wanted to scream. But now, she understood the weight of the words. You had to accept your life for what it was. You couldn't pick and prod at the mistakes you made or the reasons why. You had to sit in the here and now and acknowledge the weight of your responsibilities. You had to be whoever you were.

"I do love you, Dad," Marcy rasped.

On television, a contestant on the game show about guessing prices of everyday items suggested that a bottle of laundry detergent would cost nine dollars, which was unreasonable. Marcy laughed aloud, knowing that her father would have called him "the idiot of the year."

These were the loneliest days of Marcy's life. In her heart, she prepared for many more years just like this.

Chapter Fifteen

By Wednesday early afternoon, Elise, Malcolm, and Peter worked out the rest of the editing kinks for the film and agreed on a plan of attack for the scenes ahead. "I can't tell you how grateful I am for your help," Peter said, palming the back of his neck sheepishly. "The thing would have turned into a mangled mess without you here."

Elise wrinkled her nose, grateful that Peter had called her out to LA before he'd made a mess of the film that was, in every sense of the word, her "passion project." "Your instincts to bring me out here were good," she said. "And it's been remarkable to be back in LA for just a few days."

"You miss the place. Admit it," Peter teased, gathering up his notepads, his pens, and his backpack.

"There's so much I'll always miss about LA," Elise said wistfully, thinking again about what Brad had said about having so many potentialities for life. "But my time here is done, for now."

"For now? I'll consider that a sign that all hope is not lost," Peter joked.

Once outside, Elise hugged both Peter and Malcolm. To the side, she squeezed Malcolm's hand and said, "I'll be seeing you Saturday?"

Malcolm nodded mischievously. "Can't wait to be back on that beautiful island of yours. I just checked the weather, too. Blue skies and sixty-two."

Elise, who'd checked the weather frantically for the better part of the week, jumped a bit from the pavement of the parking lot. "Someone up there is looking out for me," she said, eyeing the sky.

"You deserve every happiness, Elise," Malcolm affirmed. "I hope you know that."

Elise bustled back into the apartment in Beverly Hills at half past two with her heart in her throat. Already, just as they'd planned, Brad had arrived and lined his suitcases up against the couch. They decided to grab the eight p.m. flight that evening, then stay in a Detroit hotel before driving back to Mackinaw the following morning. The coziness of home beckoned.

"Hey? Brad? You here?" Elise removed her purse and rushed through the apartment, which, now that they were packed to leave, had already begun to feel like someone else's, even after three very intense days as its resident.

"In here!" Brad called from the kitchen, where Elise found him eating a piece of toast with crunchy peanut butter, his eyes out the window.

Elise explained that they'd finished the work on the film for the week, which put her in the "all clear" for her upcoming wedding and honeymoon to the Bahamas. Brad congratulated her, his smile widening excitedly. The previous evening, he'd expressed joy that soon, he would leap off the Los Angeles coast and "get a break from his broken heart." Elise knew better than most that sometimes, all you needed was a bit of a different perspective on something. It made all the difference.

When Elise returned to the living room, there was a surprise email on her phone.

Elise,

Good afternoon! Apologies for the delay in my response. I've been in Barcelona on business.

I must admit that it's a pleasure for me to hear that you appreciate my work, as I'm quite familiar with yours. My wife is a long-time Elise Darby fan, and I've come to appreciate the artistry and heart of your films.

Why don't we set up a meeting? I've kept the following few days free to adjust to the time zone change. Name the time, and I can make myself available.

All the best,

Zane Hamlet

Elise's eyes widened with genuine shock. Sunday night (or, really, Monday morning), Elise had reached out to her ex-colleague and friend, on the hunt for Zane's contact. When he'd sent it back, Elise had written Zane immediately, yet hadn't fully expected a reply. Now, here it was.

It was even more of a surprise that Zane called himself something of an "Elise Darby fan." Elise's stomach twisted with a mix of joy and betrayal. After all, Marcy was a part of the beautiful texture of Elise's brand-new life, and Zane represented everything that had ever gone wrong in Marcy's life.

Elise told herself that she didn't actually have time to see Zane Hamlet before she and Brad flew out later that evening. It would make everything much too frantic.

But curiosity burned through her. Elise watched herself, as though from a great distance, as she typed out her response.

Zane,

Marvelous to hear from you. I'm headed out of town this evening, but I could make time this afternoon if you're not too far. I'm in Beverly Hills.

Elise Darby

Zane wrote back a few minutes later. The email that dinged into Elise's phone made her heart race.

Elise,

I'm on Mulholland Drive. I'd love to welcome you to my home this afternoon if you have the time. Four-thirty?

Best,

Zane

It wasn't difficult to get Brad to head to Mulholland Drive. In the rental car, Elise explained the situation to Brad about Marcy, the old blueprints, and the case of the jilted bride. "Everyone on the island is so sure that Marcy hates love," Elise said, her hands gripping the steering wheel powerfully. "But now, it's like this whole other world has opened up behind her."

"And nobody knows why he left?" Brad asked, breathless.

"Nobody," Elise affirmed. "Except for Zane himself, I'm assuming."

"Wow," Brad said, impressed. "And you tracked him down?"

"He's done really well for himself and just so happens to be well-connected to a few people in my little world," Elise explained, shifting easily into the left lane, despite the chaos of downtown Los Angeles traffic. There she was again: a Los Angeles girl, through and through. She was the sort of woman who knew what she wanted and how to get it. This was no different.

"And what do you want from him?" Brad asked, arching his brow.

Elise dragged her tongue across the back of her lower teeth, both grateful and irritated at the question. "I just want to know why someone makes a choice like that. I want to understand it. Maybe it's just like what you said the other day about the different paths we take in life. What makes us go one way and not the other?"

Brad nodded sadly, his smile waning. Since he'd spoken

about the breakup on Monday evening, he'd made a point not to mention it. Still, Elise could feel it within him as though it was a knife that remained lodged in his side.

Zane Hamlet's house on Mulholland Drive was far more understated than Elise pictured. It was a one-story home that sprawled across the hills, with a beautiful view of the valley below and encircled by several palm trees that shifted in the light breeze. When Elise announced herself, a large iron gate opened to allow her to drive through. She felt like a spy, ruffling through the details of the past.

Elise parked the rental in the driveway, and together, she and Brad stepped toward the front door, where Bethany Hamlet greeted them warmly. Bethany was in her early fifties and kept her hair chopped at her ears. On her feet, she wore cream-colored slippers, which seemed like the kind that immediately soothed sore tendons.

"Elise Darby, I can't tell you how wonderful it is to meet you," Bethany began, smiling tenderly.

"It's not every day that I meet a fan," Elise said with a soft laugh, genuinely embarrassed. "Thank you."

"Yes, well." Bethany laughed to herself, clearly just as embarrassed as Elise was. "He's in his study. I can't get him to take much more than a few hours off of work."

"My mom's the same way," Brad suggested of Elise, which made the three of them laugh as they paraded toward Zane Hamlet's study. On the way, Elise glanced around the space—taking note of the grandfather clock, the numerous antiques, the modern art paintings, and the wide collection of old scotches and whiskeys. Nothing in the space suggested that Zane Hamlet had any relation at all to the Pink Pony Bar and Grill on Mackinac Island. It amazed Elise how far he could run from the past.

Although, she supposed that she had done the same thing when she'd moved out to Mackinac.

Zane sat behind an antique desk with an expensive pencil lifted as he swept through the final lines of what looked like a blueprint. Elise imagined a much younger Zane, piecing together the blueprints for the house he'd wanted to build on Mackinac. Every line was precise and filled with purpose. And then, the blueprint had been rolled up and placed in a trunk for more than thirty years.

"Good afternoon!" Zane greeted them warmly and stood, stretching his hand across the desk. He wore a knitted blue sweater and a pair of slacks. On the desk between them, a large mug of tea sweated against a coaster. Elise shook his hand and said a number of pleasantries about his home, then introduced Brad.

"Brad has a wonderful eye for all things architecture," Elise lied. "I needed him here for the meeting."

Zane nodded, meeting Brad's gaze as he sat. "Are you in the field, Brad?"

Brad shook his head. "It was a dream of mine to become an architect. I don't know where I lost that dream along the way."

"You're still quite young," Zane said. "I always like to remind young people that they can change their minds as many times as they want to. When you're a bit older, things get complicated. Your life gets written, so to speak. But right now, you can make everything up as you go along. Unless you're married with a family?"

"Not quite," Brad said. "Just went through a breakup, actually."

Zane's face broke into a sad smile at Brad's clear honesty. "I'm sorry to hear that. I really am. I know that it can feel like your life explodes at its very core."

Elise's throat tightened as she took in the view of this man. In every sense, he seemed brave, honest, and open-hearted. *How could a man like this run out on Marcy? How could a man like this destroy a woman so completely?* Elise felt as though she studied the main character of a novel, struggling to understand what made him tick.

But how could she get to the topic of conversation fluidly? She couldn't make him feel like she'd come there to accost him. In fact, despite what she knew about his past, she rather liked him.

Zane asked that Bethany bring them tea, which she did very shortly after. As their tea bags steeped, Zane explained to Brad and Elise the work he'd been doing in Barcelona, plus the trip he had planned out to Tokyo for early November. He spoke about different cultures with specificity and excitement, yet also seemed unwilling to brag about his outrageously cool life.

"Now, tell me," Zane said, tilting his head. "You mentioned that you have a potential project for me. What sort of thing did you have in mind? Something like Benny's place, I presume?"

Elise lowered her upper teeth over her bottom lip, suddenly terrified. She glanced toward Brad, wondering if she should side-step the issue totally and just pretend that she actually did want a house like Benny's. But before she could make up her mind, Brad spoke— clearly far more interested in "the paths we take in life" given his recent breakup. He burned to understand life and its great mysteries.

"Mom just left Los Angeles, actually," Brad said, his smile secretive. "It's been a bit of a shock."

Zane's eyes widened with mock surprise. *What did he care if some woman he didn't know had moved away?* "And what called you away from our beautiful city, Elise Darby?"

Elise stuttered slightly before she finally drummed up the words. "Mackinac Island, actually."

In the split-second she said the name of her beautiful island, Zane's face transformed. The once confident and open-hearted man now looked strange and stricken, as though he'd just learned about a terrible tragedy.

Finally, he repeated the name. "Mackinac Island. Wow." He leaned back in his chair and crossed his arms over his chest, slowly filling his lungs with air. After a dramatic pause, he whispered, "I'm starting to feel like a character in one of your movies, Elise Darby."

Elise's heart pounded with intrigue. This wasn't something she'd expected him to say, yet it cleared the air slightly. He understood, in a sense, why she'd come.

"I believe I just purchased a house you might be very familiar with," Elise whispered, surprised now at her own bravery. "A very big old house on a very beautiful hill."

Zane closed his eyes, clearly swimming in wave after wave of emotion. "My family's place. Gosh. Yes. My father's realtor told me that there had been a buyer. I'd shoved all thoughts of that away, as the guilt of knowing it now belonged to someone outside of my family felt too enormous. But of course, there's no way on earth that I can go back to Mackinac."

The edges of Elise's heart cracked at the edges. Here he was, acknowledging the weight of the past.

Slowly, Brad shifted forward, his eyebrows furrowed. "What happened, Mr. Hamlet?"

Zane's eyes were glassy and far away. After a long pause, he whispered, "I don't know what you mean."

Brad lifted his shoulder. "We're not here to demonize any decision that you might have made thirty-five years ago. Actually, I can only speak for myself when I say this— but I'm here to try to understand the reasons any of us do what we do. As you said before, I'm still young. I want to understand how to build a life that I can be proud of. I want to understand how to build a life of love."

Zane pressed his lips together. For the first time, it very much looked as though he had spent the better part of the past twenty-four hours traveling from Barcelona.

"I take it she's still there," he said softly.

Elise recognized the ache behind his words. "She's still there."

Zane dropped his gaze to the desk. After a pause, he began to speak very quietly, as though he didn't want anyone else in the world to hear.

"I never told anyone what happened," he muttered. "Because it's the greatest shame of my life."

Elise and Brad kept their eyes trained on him, captivated.

"I need you both to understand that I loved Marcy more than I knew what to do with," Zane insisted, his nostrils flared. "I met her one summer in my early teenage years, and I was immediately captivated. When I wasn't on the island during the year, I wrote her letter after letter and counted down the days until we would see one another again. Summers were blissful and electric and everything that teenage summers on Mackinac Island should be. My parents were genuinely surprised that I wanted to marry a girl from Mackinac, especially Elliott Plymouth's daughter, but I insisted that that was what I wanted. Eventually, they supported me.

"Everything was set. That summer of '87, I secured a job out in Seattle, where I would start as the assistant to the junior architect at a firm. The money wasn't brilliant, but I wanted to be out in Seattle— somewhere where, I felt, 'things' happened. I'm not sure anymore what 'things' I thought happened out in Seattle, but there you are. I was young and naive and incredibly pleased with myself. Marcy was over the moon for me. I wasn't sure what she would do once we got out to Seattle, but she insisted that it didn't matter, not yet. Besides, we both seemed very sure that our love was the kind of thing that would sustain us, no matter what. It sounds foolish. But at the time, it was the only language we really understood."

Here, Zane's eyes darkened. He took a sip of tea and then lifted his pencil to flick the sharp edge against the paper.

"Obviously, I was familiar with Marcy's father, Elliott,"

Zane continued. "He thought that I was a spoiled city boy, which, I suppose, I was, especially compared to him. During those final months before the wedding, it seemed like Elliott did everything he could to stick a wedge between Marcy and I. When I got the job out in Seattle, Marcy decided not to tell him, as she felt that it would destroy him. I kept telling her that eventually, he would have to make do without her on the island. But I know that it broke her up inside. See, she'd lost her mother as a young girl, and for years, it had just been Elliott and Marcy. She cared for him far more than any young woman should have, especially given the fact that he was..."

Zane trailed off, unsure of himself. "I don't know. Abusive is maybe not the right word. But he certainly manipulated her. I hated it. It was one of the reasons that we fought. But you know, that love for her father was something I loved about her, too. She was terribly loyal to a fault. Sometimes, I wish more people in the world were like that."

After another dramatic pause, Zane continued. "The night before the wedding, I was at the house. Your house, now, I suppose, Elise." He coughed, suddenly looking terribly old. "Elliott came up the steps. He was drunk, maybe half out of his mind, I don't know. He had a shotgun with him. I don't know if it was loaded; I guess I never will. He told me to get the hell off the island, to leave his daughter alone. I guess maybe he'd found out that Marcy and I planned to leave the island for good. Who knows?"

"And you listened to him?" Brad looked stricken.

Zane closed his eyes so tightly that long, thick wrinkles formed all the way from the corners to his hairline. "At first, I told him to go home. That I didn't believe he would shoot me. And that I didn't care what happened to him after we left. But that's when he..." Zane shook his head, clearly overwhelmed. "I hate that I did this, Elise. I hate it."

Elise's throat was so tight that she could hardly breathe.

"He offered me three hundred thousand dollars," Zane continued, shivering with sorrow. "It was more money than I could even understand. I'm assuming that it was all the money he had in his account; probably, it was every single penny he'd saved since he'd opened the Pink Pony. With that money, I thought I wouldn't have to take that stupid assistant to the junior position in Seattle after all. I could move wherever I wanted to and start making real architectural advancements. I wouldn't have to prove myself as much. I could just— make it. Like that." He snapped his fingers.

Elise's lips opened with genuine surprise. Before she could answer, Zane hurried to try to explain.

"I know that it was the most selfish and evil thing I've ever done. I have lived with the guilt and the regret every single day since then. It's been a weight on my mind and my heart." Zane then gestured around the study, back toward the main house, and out the window, where they enjoyed a gorgeous view of the valley beyond. "Without Elliott Plymouth, none of this would have been possible. And I hate myself for that, every single day of my life."

Chapter Sixteen

Elise and Brad were wordless on the drive to the Los Angeles Airport. Zane's story sizzled through their minds; his constant apologies and his *"Please, find a way to see that I did this for a good reason"* had followed them out the door, even as they'd insisted that they "couldn't blame him," and that he'd been too young to fully understand the weight of what he'd done. Once Elise had dropped off the car at the rental place, she found Brad with his head down and two cups of coffee at his feet. His sigh wasn't the sigh of a twenty-two-year-old man, but of a much more exhausted human, one who understood the weight of time and the horrible things that people so often did to one another.

"He seems like such a good person," Brad said softly as he passed the cup of coffee to Elise.

Elise's cheek twitched. "Maybe he is. Maybe he's spent the rest of his life trying to make up for this one terrible thing that he did."

Brad and Elise sipped their coffees and watched the glass doors as they burst open for groups of travelers, all walking too quickly as they raced toward their flight gates. Both remained wordless, going over the events of that fateful summer in 1987. It seemed incredible that Zane had just run off with Elliott Plymouth's life savings; even more, it seemed horrific to hold that secret within them. Elise felt she might burst.

"There she is." Brad stood from the plastic chair and adjusted his posture just as his twin sister bustled through the glass, swinging two suitcases, her blond hair shining. Penny rushed toward them, her smile chaotic but endearing.

"Hi! Sorry, I'm late!"

As Penny burrowed into a group hug, she brought a wave of iconic perfume (what was it? A mix of rose and sandalwood? She would have to ask Penny later). Elise closed her eyes, overwhelmed with the love she felt for her two children.

Elise, Brad, and Penny fell into the haze of the following hour at the airport: dropping off their bags, bumping slowly through security, and finally landing at the flight gate, where Penny disappeared to grab them water bottles and little snacks. This left Elise and Brad alone again, glancing at one another contemplatively.

"I don't think I want to tell Penny about this," Brad said softly.

"You took the words right out of my mouth," Elise murmured.

"It's not that I don't trust her," Brad began.

"No. We trust her," Elise affirmed. "But I know what you mean. This story isn't ours. It doesn't belong to us. It almost feels like we never should have learned it in the first place."

When Penny returned with water and little white chocolate oatmeal cookies, she perched gently at the edge of the plastic seat and chatted graciously about the days ahead.

"I've been off the island for only nine days!" she cooed. "And already, I'm heading back."

"You're a part-time Mackinac resident at this point," Elise

teased. "I already told Brad that my dream is for the two of you to spend summers there with Wayne and I at the new place."

Penny dropped her head back so that her blond hair shifted across the upper line of her skirt. "Don't you remember? I spent weeks there over last summer and let some Mackinac boy break my heart."

"Mackinac seems like a dangerous place for hearts," Brad said, his eyes glittering knowingly.

Penny dropped her upper teeth over her lip and then whispered, "Gosh, I'm so sorry about your recent..."

Brad waved a hand, clearly not wanting to get into the logistics of his recent breakup. "It's cool. Really."

"It's not," Penny insisted. "But we don't have to talk about it. This week is all about celebrating Mom and Wayne."

"It's not just about that," Elise said, stitching her brows together. "It's about us coming together as a family. It's about the two of you being a part of this next phase of my life. Being a mother was and is the single greatest achievement in my life. Now that the two of you are twenty-two, I'm so grateful to enter this new era with you."

"The era of us being very confused young adults?" Brad joked.

Elise laughed knowingly. "There is no era of life that isn't confusing. I hope that together, we can learn to enjoy the ride a little bit."

* * *

The flight back to Detroit was joyful and unforgettable. Throughout, Elise, Penny, and Brad sipped champagne and chatted about Elise's film, Elise's final few days in Los Angeles, and, of course, the wedding celebrations ahead. As the plane fled across the continent and into the night, Elise tried to step back from the drama of Marcy and Zane's final days together in

1987 and into the glimmering excitement of her future with Wayne on Mackinac.

The plane landed around midnight. Bleary-eyed, Elise, Penny, and Brad stepped into a quiet and dull airport, one with darkened restaurants and shops with their doors latched shut. To save time, they checked into the hotel that was attached to the airport and soon fell into the welcome embrace of sleep in a double room— with Penny and Brad in two double beds and Elise in a queen in the next room. When she woke up the following morning, only two days before her wedding, Michigan sunlight flooded into the room between the unclosed curtains, and a bright blue sky stretched over the whole of the state. As she sipped her coffee, Elise checked the weather app on her phone for proof. Sure enough, the weather for Saturday still held strong— sixty-two degrees and sunny.

Elise drove her children back up to Mackinaw City that morning, parked the car in the long-term parking garage, and soon found herself on the top deck of Shepler's Ferry, waving hello to the captain, Kurt. As it was late in October and a weekday, the ferry was mostly empty, its long lines of plastic chairs void of the tourists that had filled them all summer long

"It's eerie," Penny said, flipping her hair beneath her winter hat. "The island just sort of closes down, doesn't it?"

"But people will be arriving like crazy tomorrow," Brad reminded her. "Wedding guests, that is."

"That's right." Kurt stepped toward them as the boat motored across the Straits of Mackinac. "The boats will be filled with Elise and Wayne's loved ones, and that's about it."

Elise laughed and introduced Kurt to Brad, calling him "Shepler's number-one captain." "Oh, but he's a man of many hats," Elise continued. "He's a part-time bartender at the Pink Pony and part-time carriage driver for bachelorette parties."

"I'm retired from carriage driving for bachelorette parties," Kurt joked.

As Kurt headed back to the captain's station, Elise's heart swelled against her ribcage. Kurt was Marcy's dearest friend, a frequent employee, and the only one who seemed capable of making her smile at the drop of a hat. *What did Kurt know of Zane Hamlet? Had Kurt been around during that time?*

As the ferry drifted closer to the Mackinac Island docks, a familiar figure stepped toward the edge. He wore a thick flannel and a pair of jeans, and his dark locks wafted in the breeze, thick and wild. Elise wrapped her hands around the railing on the top deck of the ferry and met his gaze, mouthing the only words she knew were true. "I love you." In return, Wayne mouthed, "I love you, too." The Mackinac winds whipped between them.

Once on land, Wayne tugged Penny's and Elise's suitcases behind him, chatting easily with Brad about the flight. Elise and Penny brought up the rear, smiling as they marched down Main Street. Several islanders stepped out of coffee shops or local stores and waved at Elise, brimming with happiness for the weekend ahead. An older woman who worked as a seamstress several streets away leaned against her cane and sang, "Here comes the bride," her voice genuine and rasping.

It was just past two in the afternoon, and already, a steady stream of customers lined up outside the Pink Pony, their cheeks lifted to the sunlight as they ate sandwiches or chicken wings and sipped light beers. As Elise passed, she caught sight of Marcy behind the bar counter, her hand pressing against the beer tap as she filled yet another pint. Elise struggled to make eye contact with Marcy to send her a smile. But before Marcy glanced up, Elise had already passed her by.

Elise could only imagine the expectation and promise that Marcy had had during the days leading up to her wedding to Zane. *Where had Marcy put all that love? Had it simply exploded within her, leaving her a shell of her former self?*

That afternoon, Dean welcomed Penny, Brad, Elise, and

Wayne up at his house, where they ate burgers and salads, sipped wine, and sat in the splendor of the orange afternoon light. When they could, Emma, Tracey, Cindy, Michael, and Margot all came by. Margot carried little Winnie against her chest, beaming with joy. Tracey reported that she'd seen the wedding cake at the downtown bakery and that the baker had knocked it out of the park. Emma brimmed with enthusiasm, saying that Megan was on her way back up from Michigan State for the wedding. "She already got her driver's license," Cindy said proudly. "And bought herself a used car so she can come back and forth whenever she pleases."

For dinner, Cindy baked them cheese and chicken enchiladas and poured another round of wine. Wayne's sister had arrived with her children, and everyone spoke excitedly, already in celebration-mode. Elise found herself caught up in it all, bursting with laughter and goodwill. How had she gotten so lucky to have so much love in her life? What had she done to deserve any of it?

Around eleven that night, all the twenty-somethings had taken refuge in a separate room, swapping stories and pouring more drinks. Wayne's sister had gone, as had Cindy and Tracey. Dean reported that he was "too tired to stand up," which left Elise and Wayne to wrap themselves up in their jackets and scarves and head home. Both Penny and Brad would stay up at Dean's, where they had separate bedrooms and enough space to spread out. On top of that, Elise knew that her father adored having his "new" grandchildren around, especially the ones from California. As a Midwestern man, people from all corners of the outside world excited him, and he'd made it a habit of learning everything he could about the world in which Penny and Brad had grown up.

When Elise and Wayne reached their little house down the hill, Wayne admitted that he was "beat." Elise, however, still sizzled with adrenaline.

"For me, it's still eight o'clock at night," Elise said, reminding Wayne of the time difference between Michigan and California.

"Right." Wayne laughed and kissed her delicately on the cheek. "You'll need that energy tomorrow and Saturday. Why don't you save it?"

"I think I'm just going to go for a walk," Elise said. "Clear my head a little."

Wayne arched his brow, his face opening with curiosity and fear. "Do I have a runaway bride on my hands?"

Elise shook her head almost violently; her hair wafted across her cheeks. Quickly, she lifted onto her toes and kissed Wayne tenderly, her eyes closed. "You have nothing to worry about. I promise you that."

Once outside, Elise shoved her hands in her pockets and made a beeline toward the Pink Pony. From the street, the Pink Pony continued to buzz with several locals and tourists, all of whom sipped their drinks till the one a.m. closing time. Elise drew the door open and stepped out from the sharp chill and into the warm energy of the little bar, a space she'd taken for granted during her early days on Mackinac. In every way, the Pink Pony was a meeting point, a space where all islanders came together to swap stories, share gossip, and celebrate life moments, big and small. Marcy maintained the heartbeat of Mackinac.

Marcy stood on the other side of the bar with a large metal straw whipping through what looked like a hot toddy. Her smile, cast across the bar toward Elise, didn't quite meet her eyes. How exhausting it must have been, Elise thought now, to return to this bar, day after day, and pretend to be happy.

"Hi, Marcy!" Elise said as she slipped onto a stool at the bar.

"There she is," Marcy said. "The bride-to-be."

"Here I am." Elise returned and then knocked her knuckles against the countertop.

"What can I get for you?" Marcy asked.

"Just a glass of chardonnay. When you have the time."

Marcy bowed her head, delivered the hot toddy, then waved goodbye to the table of five that now departed, leaving the bar softer, slower. Elise glanced around to realize that it was now just her and two other couples, both of whom spoke sparingly and watched the television screens on high.

"How was it out in LA?" Marcy asked, eyeing Elise curiously as she washed the beer glasses in the sink.

"Oh! You knew I was gone? I guess that's not a surprise. You always seem to know what everyone is up to on this island," Elise said.

Marcy lifted a shoulder mischievously. "Not so much else to do around here but get in other people's business. You've been on the island long enough to know that."

"I suppose you're right." Elise sipped her wine. In the silence that followed, first one couple, then another took their leave from the bar, waving goodbye to Marcy as they went. "You should be able to close early tonight," Elise suggested, eyeing the empty bar.

"Gosh, I hope so," Marcy said, rubbing her temples. For the first time, Elise acknowledged just how tired Marcy looked, as though she carried the weight of the world on her shoulders.

"I'll get through this wine quickly. Don't worry," Elise said with a wry smile.

Marcy splayed a rag across the counter, scrubbing at a sticky spot. "No rush, Elise. I imagine that you have a great deal on your mind right now. Marriage is no small thing, or so I'm told."

Elise tilted her head, her tongue burning. Why had she come to the Pink Pony that night? Had she expected to tell

Marcy what she'd learned about her father and Zane's betrayal? Had she expected to support Marcy in some way?

"I can't help but press you for information, Marcy," Elise said suddenly, her voice bouncing.

Marcy arched her brow. "Regarding?"

"The issue of the missing RSVP," Elise said, leaning across the bar. "I told you already, I would love to have you at my wedding. I'd especially love to pay other bartenders to serve you drinks, for once."

"Imagine that. Me, having a good time?" Marcy joked wryly, in a way that showed just how exhausted she truly was.

"Let me help you with those tables," Elise said, leaping up to grab the other rag in a little bucket of suds and water.

"Honey, you don't have to do that."

"Come on. I'm jet-lagged with a million little things to worry about," Elise admitted. "Letting me help you is doing me a favor."

Marcy shrugged. "Suit yourself." She then scrubbed through the rest of the beer glasses, clinking them up side-by-side to dry across the drying rack. Elise worked diligently, jumping from one table to another until she finished and reached for the broom in the corner. When she had the broom in her hands, she lifted her gaze to find Marcy studying her. It was as though Marcy had never really looked at her before. The gaze was fiery, stunning. Elise tried to imagine this woman in the mansion on Mulholland Drive, hurrying away to make Zane a cup of tea. It was difficult. The pieces didn't fit.

Suddenly, before Elise's eyes, Marcy's face crumpled. A sob of exhaustion swelled from her throat as she fell forward, dropping her face in her hands. Elise returned the broom to the corner and hurried behind the bar, placing her hand on Marcy's upper back. Sob after sob came from Marcy's little body, each louder than the one before it.

"Hey. It's okay. Marcy, it's okay." Elise tried to speak to

Marcy the way she'd once spoken to her children when they'd cried. This time, however, she wasn't entirely sure if everything was "okay." How could she tell a broken woman that everything would be all right? How could she paint a picture of optimism?

"I'm so sorry," Marcy sputtered, reaching for a package of Kleenex on the counter. "Gosh, I feel like a fool."

Elise stepped back, recognizing that Marcy needed space. "You have nothing to apologize for."

Marcy sniffed and blew her nose, her cheeks blossoming into pinks and reds. "No. I just." She shook her head, hunting for the right words. "I've had a hard week, I suppose. My father had a stroke."

Elise's heart dropped into her belly. "Oh, Marcy. I'm so sorry." Her thoughts spun with horror.

"It's okay. Or, it's not okay, but it will be." Marcy closed her eyes to show the pinks of her eyelids. "He can't speak right now, but the doctor says that he probably will be able to soon. A few years ago, I put him in a nursing home out in Cheboygen, which has been good for both of us. We've lived together our entire lives and just needed space. But I can't help but feel guilty, you know? The man has always been a snake. Always! And yet, he's the only family I've ever had. I love him to pieces. What else can I say? I've always been too loyal to him; I know that. But I also don't know what I'll do when I lose him. It's been a huge reminder of just how alone I actually am."

Elise closed her eyes against the agony of the situation. Although she didn't know what Elliott Plymouth looked like, she had a very clear image of a much younger man standing before Zane with a shotgun and three hundred thousand dollars on offer— all in exchange to leave his daughter alone. Now, that man couldn't speak. *How selfish he was! How selfish Zane was!* And here Marcy was, weeping and alone at the bar she'd been left with.

It struck Elise that she couldn't tell Marcy any of this. How could she tell this woman that the father she so desperately loved had ruined her life? It would be like pulling the rug out from under her.

Elise closed the distance between herself and Marcy. Marcy's eyes were wounded and enormous, clinging to tears that she wouldn't let fall. Finally, Elise wrapped her arms around her, dropped her chin onto her shoulder, and whispered, "You're not alone, you know? And you're so deserving of love from all of us. We need you, Marcy."

"Yeah. Everyone needs me to refill their beers."

Elise laughed, surprised at Marcy's ever-present sarcasm and witticism. She pulled back slightly and met Marcy's gaze. "We need you for your friendship, for your listening ear, and for your overwhelming support. You're one of the heartbeats of this island. Don't you dare forget that."

Chapter Seventeen

The alarm clock blared on Marcy's cell. As she was already two and a half miles into her run by then, Marcy stabbed the screen of her phone to stop the alarm clock, adjusted her posture, and continued to flee around the island, which was a trek she'd made countless times. The full circumference of the island was nine miles, which was deemed "very small" by people who couldn't run around it. Marcy only bothered to go the full round when she felt especially determined— or especially sorrowful. Something about stretching her legs as the morning swelled around her reignited her passion for life. Something about the sharp chill of the air and the shimmering waters beyond the shores made her remember that there was so much more to live for.

Marcy had only returned back from Cheboygen the previous morning, hoping that a bit of normality in the form of a bar shift would make her feel more like herself. Unfortunately, the endless barrage of beers to fill and cocktails to mix had only dropped her deeper into a depression. The text message she'd sent to Kurt, announcing that she'd returned from Cheboygen, remained unanswered. Increasingly, she was beginning to wonder just how much she'd messed up her life. Now that she'd pushed Kurt away for good, she'd begun to dream about running off to build a new life elsewhere.

But who was Marcy Plymouth? Who would she be in this other place? It wasn't like she could just step off a plane some-where and automatically learn how to form friendships. She'd spent her life alone with her father, with Kurt. Mackinac was all she knew. Was she kidding herself, dreaming about elsewhere?

Last night, Marcy made a grave error. She'd told Elise Darby about her ailing father, about her loneliness. In return, Elise had held her as though Marcy was a small child, adrift in a world she couldn't understand. Marcy hated how much she'd loved being held. She hated that it had felt so wonderful to be cared for.

Was that the sort of love and affection that other people enjoyed every single day? Was that what she had been missing all these years? The idea of all those missed hugs filled her with a longing that she couldn't understand. In response, she picked up her speed and began to sprint through miles four, five, and six like her life depended on it. Maybe it did.

When Marcy finished her run, she stopped near the ferry docks, gasping for breath. The past hour and fifteen minutes had passed swiftly. She hung her fingers near her toes, feeling the arch of her spine and thinking about the day ahead. Elise had pushed her to be a guest at her wedding to Wayne, but Marcy was resistant. She'd made good on her promise to herself never to attend a wedding. *What made Elise any different?*

When Marcy lifted up from her stretch, she peered out across the docks, her eyes watering against the chill of the air. To her surprise, a very familiar sailboat creaked against the far dock, its mast pointing to the bright blue sky above.

Marcy had spent many hours of her life on that very boat. It was perhaps the only boat she truly knew how to sail, as Kurt had pushed her to learn, manipulating the sails and the ropes in a way that allowed them to cut evenly through the billowing waves.

A split-second later, Kurt's head jumped up from below deck. After that, the swell of his broad back glowed beneath the October sun. Marcy leaped toward him, feeling hungry for something she couldn't fully understand. One thing she knew was this: Kurt deserved an apology. He was the only friend she had in the world— and she couldn't afford to give up on what they had.

Marcy stood before Kurt's boat, her chest rising and falling. It was only then that it occurred to her that she was slick with sweat from her nine-mile run. Then again, this was Kurt. Kurt had seen her in every physical state. He didn't care what she looked like. He knew her heart; he knew her mind; he knew her spirit.

When he finally turned back to find her there, Kurt jumped in surprise. His eyes glistened with recognition, but his lips remained flat and unsmiling.

"Marcy," he breathed her name.

Marcy squeezed the sweaty fabric of her shorts. "Kurt." Why had she never noticed just how delicious his name sounded across her tongue? How many times had she said his name before? *Millions of times? Billions?*

"I'm sorry that I didn't write you back," Kurt offered, palming his neck.

Marcy's nostrils flared. Honesty was a thing she didn't fully understand. "I'm sorry that I..." She trailed off. "I'm just sorry."

Internally, her thoughts ran wild: *I'm sorry that I kicked you out of Cheboygen when I really needed you. That I've never been able to appreciate you the way I should have. That I've never known how to love you.*

After a dramatic pause, Kurt stepped up on the dock, his

eyes still glistening. His body was muscular and thick and only about two feet away. Marcy had the sudden desire to wrap her arms around his waist and dig her face into his chest. God, she'd missed him.

But it was Kurt's turn to speak. "I hope you know that I just want to be there for you. I just want to help you. I know that things are and have always been complicated with your father. But you deserve far more than he's ever give you."

Marcy's lower lip quivered with sorrow. "I don't know how to accept that."

"You have to learn," Kurt whispered, his voice breaking.

Marcy shook her head, overwhelmed. "How does anyone learn how to do that?"

Kurt bridged the distance between them and took her delicate hand in his. Marcy wanted to protest and tell him just how "disgusting" she was, especially after her run. She wanted to say that she'd been pretty once, maybe— but all that was in the past. If Kurt wanted to, he could flee the island, meet a younger woman, and maybe even have a baby or two. If she was a true friend to Kurt, she would have told him that.

"Why don't you have a coffee with me?" Kurt whispered, tilting his head toward his boat. "Out on the water?"

Marcy blinked down at her sweat-stained clothes, ready to protest. Before she could, Kurt said, "You know, I think you're the most beautiful woman on this island. I always have. Sweat stains and all."

Marcy's cheeks burned with embarrassment. She fumbled around her emotions without any clear understanding of them. After a pause, she felt herself nod to his question about coffee, and she followed him onto the boat, watching as he easily untied the ropes, whipped open the sails, and brought the boat out onto the glistening Straits. As she was chilly, her clothes stained with sweat, Kurt suggested that she head downstairs to the berth to change into a pair of clean sweats and wrap herself in a blanket. When she emerged back to the deck, Kurt had a pot of coffee ready, along with a platter of freshly baked croissants, which he'd picked up from The Grind.

The image of Kurt, there waiting with croissants and coffee as the winds off the Straits billowed through his hair, would remain with Marcy for the rest of her days. It was at this moment that she realized the depths of her love for him. It was at this moment that she fully knew what it meant to give her life to another.

As she sat next to him, clutching the mug of freshly brewed coffee, she whispered a question that surprised her.

"Maybe this is out of left field. But would you like to go to a wedding with me this weekend? I really need a date."

Kurt's surprise echoed out from his handsome face. He sipped his coffee, seeming to treasure this moment. Then, he said, "I can't think of anything else in the world I'd rather do."

Chapter Eighteen

E lise's mother, Allison Darby, had always made her opinions about marriage known. Throughout the early years of Elise's time with Sean, Allison had muttered with slight exasperation, saying, *"I don't know why you think you need a man to do any of this,"* while she assisted with all the ins and outs of mothering a pair of twins. During that time, Sean had insisted that he required space and time alone to ensure that his newfound career would flourish. This, Elise knew, had taken time away from her own career— and ultimately sent her screenwriting days into a downward spiral.

On the morning of October 22nd, Elise awoke upon glittering white sheets in the bridal suite at the Grand Hotel, the very hotel where Allison Darby and Dean Swartz had met to continue their affair back in the summer of 1979. The hotel was the single most romantic place on the island, a beacon of history, with its old-fashioned dining rooms, its gorgeous and sweeping grounds, and its world-famous porch, which tourists actually paid to sit on during the summer. The Grand Hotel had been an obvious choice for Elise's marriage to Wayne— but the reality of waking up there, so many decades after her mother had slept there with Dean Swartz, split Elise's heart in two. How she wished that her mother could be there!

Elise sat at the edge of the bed in a white nightgown and studied her toes, which she'd had pedicured the previous afternoon, together with Penny, Cindy, Tracey, Emma, and Megan. The previous evening had been a whirlwind of events, with fifty-five people arriving on the island for pre-wedding festivities, plus drinks and dinner. Wayne and Elise had done their best to welcome everyone, putting in face time with as many as they could before collapsing, exhausted, in their dinner chairs and tucking in a beautiful salmon meal.

"Mom?" Penny's sweet voice echoed out from the hallway, followed by a light tapping against the door.

Elise rose and walked like a ghost to discover her beautiful daughter, still with sleep in her eyes. Penny held two cups of coffee in her hands, and her blond hair spilled down her back, still unkempt after sleeping. Elise welcomed her in, aching to see Allison Darby's face across her daughter's. That was life, Elise knew. It came in cycles.

"I couldn't sleep anymore," Penny admitted as she sat with her mother. "I kept thinking of Grandma. About how much I wish she was here to see you marry Wayne."

Elise's heart lifted. "I was thinking of her, too." This seemed proof of something, as though the heaven where Allison Darby resided wasn't so far from where they were now. Elise had to hope so, at least.

"She would have loved him," Penny said, mostly to her toes. "But most of all, she would have loved the way he's opened you up again. Since you met Wayne, an entire script poured out of you. And after that, the script was immediately filmed. I mean, above everything, Grandma appreciated the hard work that creativity calls for. She drilled that into me over and over again when I told her that I wanted to be an actress."

"Your grandmother was not lazy," Elise affirmed, her heart straining in her chest.

"It's so funny to get to know Grandpa better," Penny continued, tilting her head. "I can understand why Grandma fell for him. Although I have to admit, I don't think it ever would have worked between them. She was far too driven. And Dean..."

"He's a bit too contemplative for her," Elise agreed, having had the same thought several times.

"I guess it goes to show that sometimes, people love one another without rhyme or reason," Penny affirmed.

"And I'm not sure that anyone ever gets the system exactly right," Elise breathed. After another sip of coffee, she stood and walked toward the window to watch as the morning light played out across the sweeps of green gardens, still manicured despite the lateness of the year. "But I sure as heck hope that I'm getting it right with Wayne."

Elise again thought of Marcy and Zane— of Marcy's belief that Zane was her ever-after and about Zane's ability to throw her away with the first sign of money. Elise had to hope that Wayne wasn't the sort of man to do that. *But how could anyone ever truly know?* Love was a gamble. That's what made it so special.

A little while later, Tracey, Emma, Megan, and Cindy arrived with bottles of champagne, freshly squeezed orange juice, and little flute glasses meant for mimosas. As Penny turned on a lovely little morning playlist, with tracks like "Come Away With Me" and "This Could Be," Tracey mixed up the morning cocktails and explained that the hairdressers and makeup artists were on their way. By three that afternoon, the women would be prepared for photographs; at four-thirty, Elise and Wayne would be married. The day would be a whirlwind of emotion, of champagne, of laughter, and of cake, but right then, surrounded by the women she loved most, Elise felt the world grow still. Here, she could appreciate everything she had.

"It's just so hard to believe." Tracey blubbered as she sipped her champagne, her gaze toward the cerulean sky. "You waltzed into our lives just last year and completely turned everything on its head."

Elise laughed. "Don't give me that much credit. I mostly came in like a bulldozer, not understanding the mess I was making."

Cindy gave Elise a rueful look. "I know it wasn't easy at the beginning. But you've brought so much love into our lives. And..." Here, she paused, searching for the right words. "I know I struggled at first about Wayne moving on. But now, seeing the happiness that you've brought into his life makes me understand how necessary all that was. Tara needs Wayne to be happy. Just like I need my half-sister to be happy." Cindy's forehead wrinkled slightly; it was clear that she worried she'd said the wrong thing.

But Elise knew that everything said that day was directly from the heart. She leaped to her feet and wrapped her arms around Cindy, marveling at the weight of Cindy's words. Cindy had been the Maid of Honor at Tara and Wayne's wedding twenty years ago; now, here she was with her heart on her sleeves at Elise and Wayne's. All Elise could do was open her heart to the memories of the ones she loved.

The photography session whisked Elise, Wayne, Wayne's small family, Penny, Brad, and the rest of the Swartz family around the gorgeous grounds of The Grand Hotel. Although every-one's cheeks were strained from smiling, nobody dared complain. Laughter rolled out of them, echoing across the grounds. The photographer suggested that they were the happiest family she'd photographed in a long while. At this, Wayne pressed his lips against Elise's cheek spontaneously before whispering, "You bring the light out of everyone. Don't you forget that."

A man of many talents, Dean Swartz had admitted several months back that he was registered to marry people in the State of Michigan. It was surreal for Elise, who walked down the aisle arm-in-arm with Brad, to approach the man she now knew was her father— a man whose face echoed with stoicism as she approached. Dean wore a simple tuxedo and had styled his beard with hints of oil. He no longer looked like the scraggly flannel-wearing man who lived on the hill. Rather, he looked straight from a magazine about men's fashion.

Wayne stepped up beside Dean, brimming with impossible happiness. As Elise turned to face him, he mouthed, "I love you," and warmth rushed through Elise's chest and through her arms. Elise mouthed it back, her eyes filling with tears. As they adjusted themselves, the string quintet quieted, and Penny and Brad shifted off to stand behind Elise, supporting her. "Bridesmaids" had been out of the question for Elise, as all she'd wanted in the world was to have her children there beside her.

"Good afternoon," Dean welcomed the crowd of over one hundred out-of-towners and islanders, which in LA wedding terms was "rather small." Elise had wanted it that way.

"We are gathered here today to join in holy matrimony two people who are very near and dear to my heart," Dean continued, his hands clasped in front of him. "I've known Wayne Tanton for many decades now. As a youngster, I thought him to be wild and alive and inherently true to himself, something that I, as an older man, craved in my own life. Wayne, you've hit some road bumps on this game of life; we know, and we recognize that here today— that in order to find happiness again, you've had to welcome it back into your life." Dean's eyes twinkled knowingly as he nodded toward an important element of his and Wayne's relationship. Both Dean and Wayne were widowers and had helped one another limp through the terror of losing a spouse. Elise was grateful to Dean for wrapping Wayne up in love, especially during Wayne's loneliest years.

"Elise Darby stepped onto Mackinac Island a little more than a year ago," Dean continued, his voice rasping with emotion. "At the time, she brought a whirlwind of gossip and chaos, which caused many not to trust her. But of course, during that first week here, she stumbled into none other than Wayne Tanton, who recognized the sort of woman she was. Wayne has expressed to me that he 'knew' she was special within the first ten minutes of talking to her. After that, he went on to help her through a very difficult patch in her life, one that ultimately led her to find me, her long-lost dad, along with her two sisters and brother. Elise, you're a remarkable part of our family here on Mackinac Island, and we are blessed that you decided to make our island your home. Wayne, we are blessed beyond measure to welcome you into the Swartz fold, although I have to admit, I've thought of you as part of my family for many years already. It's nice to make it official."

Across the sweeping green fields of The Grand Hotel, not a single onlooker had a dry eye. Wayne's large hands clutched Elise's tenderly. A soft, chilly breeze crept across the gardens and ruffled through Elise's blond strands. There, in the shadow of the enormous hotel, Dean asked Wayne and Elise to speak the vows that would unite them as man and wife for the rest of there days. And there, Wayne and Elise slid marital rings over one another's fourth fingers and fell into a passionate kiss, one that made each and every person in the audience leap to their feet with joy. There was something about watching true love play out in front of you. It was a reminder that anything in the world was possible— as long as you opened your heart to it.

Chapter Nineteen

As Elise and Wayne rushed back down the aisle, their hands clasped and their faces illuminated with joy, Marcy and Kurt exploded with applause. Marcy's face was taut and aching from too much smiling, and she dotted at her cheek with an old handkerchief that had belonged to her father, praying her tears hadn't made her makeup bleed too badly. When Kurt turned back toward her, his claps dying out, he blinked back tears of his own and pressed his lips against her cheek. The touch of his lips against her skin felt overwhelming, and Marcy shifted uneasily on her tiny heels (which were far taller than anything else she'd worn in her life). When his lips broke from her cheek, Kurt whispered, "Thank you for bringing me here today. I think I needed to see something like that. Something magical."

Marcy's lower lip quivered dangerously. Slowly, she dropped her forehead on Kurt's chest and listened to the sturdy beat of his heart. He placed both hands on her shoulders to steady her, whispering, "It's going to be all right," over and over again, as the crowd stirred around them, headed back to grab cocktails before the wedding reception officially began.

Marcy and Kurt had arrived at the wedding about fifteen minutes before anyone else. Marcy's anxious thought had been that if she'd sat and become immediately overcome with horrible memories about Zane, she could casually slip back out of the Grand Hotel grounds and be back at the Pink Pony by five before anyone noticed. Fortunately, she'd made it through.

Marcy and Kurt paraded behind the rest of the guests, exiting the seating area and joining everyone at high-top tables with white tablecloths. Marcy claimed a table while Kurt disappeared to grab them both cocktails. Several islanders passed, waving at Marcy and complimenting her dress. None of them mentioned that they'd never seen her so dressed up before. Several even said, "It's nice to see you somewhere besides behind the bar, Marcy." Marcy's heart swelled painfully. Here she was, a part of the world in a way she hadn't been since the age of twenty-one. Why had she given up on it for so long?

While she waited, Marcy watched the back of Kurt's head as he shifted forward in the cocktail line. Since she'd asked him to be her date to Elise's wedding, he'd hardly left her side Friday night, they'd worked tirelessly behind the Pink Pony bar, just like old times. Afterward, they'd collapsed upstairs in Marcy's bed— careful to keep to their separate sides. Kurt didn't want to scare Marcy away too quickly, which Marcy appreciated in her bones. Love was a tricky thing for almost anyone, but for Marcy, it was a foreign language in an ancient dialect. It would take her some time.

Back in 1987, when a friend of Marcy's had rushed into the back room at the church to tell her that Zane was "nowhere to be found," Marcy had sat in the silence of herself and watched the shadows of the day play out across the far wall. The poofy sleeves of her wedding dress had become monstrous and Halloween-y; her shoes had been too tight, and her hair had reeked of too much hairspray. No wonder Zane had left her, she'd thought; she looked like a clown.

Finally, footsteps had echoed down the hallway to bring the familiar yet anxious face of Kurt. There he'd stood, twenty-one years of muscle and sturdy shoulders and wild hair from his hours of captaining the Mackinac ferries. He'd leaned against the doorframe of that little room in the back of the church and showed off the only wedding presents a jilted bride ever really needed: a big bottle of wine and two glasses.

There they'd sat, the jilted bride and her best friend, drinking wine as a David Bowie vinyl spun around the record player. It was impossible to remember what they'd spoken about. Marcy remembered, at some point, that she'd stood and ripped the fabric of her dress from her shoulders. Kurt had howled, clapping his hands as she'd stood in expensive rags.

"What the hell am I supposed to do now, Kurt?" she'd demanded, half-laughing through tears. "I mean, is there a how-to manual I can buy about what to do when your fiancé leaves you at the altar?"

Suddenly, in the year 2022, Kurt appeared at the high top with two cocktails and that same handsome smile. Marcy thanked him and wrapped her hands around the cocktail. She wanted to ask him what had taken them so long to get to this point; she wanted to ask him what it had been like to watch her waste thirty-five years of her life.

Then again, she was tired of asking questions. It was time to live.

Marcy and Kurt were seated at a beautiful table in the dining room of The Grand Hotel, which they shared with a man named Malcolm, whom Marcy remembered from the summertime.

"Weren't you that hot-shot director?" Marcy said, snapping her fingers.

The director lifted his hands. "Guilty as charged."

"You came into the Pink Pony pretty frequently," Kurt remembered.

"Often with Miss Tracey Swartz," Marcy said with a smile.

Malcolm rubbed the back of his neck anxiously. If Marcy wasn't mistaken, Malcolm and Tracey's romantic love currently seemed impossible, given circumstances in Malcolm's life that were out of his control. How she wanted to take both Malcolm and Tracey by the hand and tell them how little time they truly had!

"Speak of the devil." Malcolm lifted his face to smile at Tracey as she approached, drawing her hair behind her ears nervously. She sat in the empty chair beside Malcolm and glanced toward Marcy before saying, "You were talking about me?"

"Only fantastic things, darling," Marcy affirmed.

Tracey's eyes glittered knowingly. After a dramatic pause, she caught Malcolm's gaze and whispered, "It's just so surreal to see you back on the island."

Malcolm nodded. "I got the rest of the week off. If you just so happen to have a bit of time to spare."

Tracey's lips parted with surprise. As the moment was too intimate, too uniquely theirs, Marcy forced her eyes back toward Kurt, who wore a wry smile. Under his breath, he whispered, "You know the ins and outs of the gossip in this town better than your own hand."

Marcy winced and laughed at once. "Guilty."

"But I have a hunch that you and I are going to give these people something to gossip about," Kurt teased.

Marcy dropped her head back, her stomach tightening with laughter. Why didn't this frighten her? For years, all she'd wanted was to be left alone. Now? She wanted to be a part of it all.

Suddenly, Dean Swartz's voice buzzed in from the microphone. He stood in the center of the dance floor with his hand extended, beaming with pride as he said, "Ladies and gentlemen, I'd like to introduce you to Wayne Tanton and Elise Darby Tanton— husband and wife!" To this, the crowd roared with applause, watching as Elise walked tenderly alongside her sturdy husband and wrapped her arms around his neck. In the center of the room, they shifted gently in time to their first dance song, "Your Song," by Elton John.

Marcy watched, captivated, her heart in her throat. Softly, Kurt bent to whisper some of the lyrics in her ear, which made a shiver race up and down her spine.

"I hope you don't mind that I put down in words how wonderful life is now you're in the world."

Marcy's eyes lifted toward Kurt's. In another reality, she might have called him sappy or overly romantic. But instead, she bridged the space between their lips, closed her eyes, and kissed him fully for the very first time. As everyone around them watched Elise and Wayne, nobody glanced in Marcy and Kurt's direction. Kurt's lips were initially tight with surprise, but they soon loosened, making space for hers. It was a surprise to learn that Marcy still "had it in her" after so many years without practice. A million emotions raced through her: surprise and heartache and pleasure and optimism and love.

When the kiss broke, Marcy whispered, "I hope that wasn't too bad?"

But Kurt shivered with laughter, wrapped his arms around her, and exhaled all the air from his lungs. "You know it was all I've wanted for decades, Marcy. It was even better than my wildest dreams."

Later, Elise and Wayne cut the cake, and the wedding servers whisked through the crowd to place a perfectly sliced piece in front of each guest. Beneath the table, Marcy and Kurt continued to hold hands as, across from them, Malcolm and Tracey stared into one another's eyes, lost in conversation.

They spoke so quietly that Marcy struggled to make out just what they said and soon gave up, as she was too invested in her own love story. Very soon after, Emma, Tracey's daughter, appeared to kiss her mother on the cheek and say, "I'm exhausted. I think I'd better head home."

"Would you like me to go with you?" Tracey asked, her voice soft and sweet.

Emma eyed Malcolm knowingly. "No, Mom. Stay here. Have a beautiful night." With her hand on her pregnant stomach, she added, "I'm not the party animal I once was."

As Emma slipped back into the chilly night, Kurt asked Marcy for a dance. Feeling a part of a dream, she clasped his hand and allowed him to lead her to the center of the dance floor, where she pressed her head against his chest and danced with him slowly, their bodies swaying in time to the music.

So many times, Marcy demanded of herself: *How did I get so lucky?* But she didn't have an answer for it. She supposed nobody ever knew why anything happened to them.

A soft tap on Marcy's shoulder made her turn. There, Elise Darby Tanton stood with a beautiful smile on her face. Since Thursday night, when Marcy had broken down and told Elise about her father's stroke, Marcy had felt a kinship with Elise that she couldn't fully understand.

"I'm so glad you could make it," Elise said. "You too, Kurt."

Kurt bowed his head. "I even changed out of the captain uniform for the ceremony."

"That must have been tough." Elise's laughter was like music. She met Marcy's gaze and lowered her voice to add, "You'll let me know if you need anything. Anything at all. Remember, we're friends on this island." She then reached out, her wedding ring flashing as she squeezed Marcy's hand.

To Marcy's surprise, she heard herself answer, "I'll let you know." She then tilted her head back toward Kurt, adding,

"Thank you for reminding me that there just might be more to life than I ever thought."

Elise's eyes sparkled. "We all need to be reminded of that every once in a while. I know that I do."

The night continued on until a little past one, at which time Kurt and Marcy walked down a pitch-black downtown street, all wrapped in one another's arms to shield them from the cold. After they stumbled into the apartment above the Pink Pony, Kurt poured Marcy a glass of water and urged her to drink.

"How many times have I poured water for people at the Pony?" Marcy stuttered with a laugh. "You're the only one who ever does it for me."

Kurt removed his dark orange autumn hat and smoothed his messy hair with the flat of his hand. "I'll take care of you, Marcy. I'll do it for the rest of my life if you'll let me."

Chapter Twenty

The following week, Kurt convinced Marcy to close the Pink Pony for several days. Deep in Marcy's bones, she was hesitant, sensing that Elliott Plymouth would run around the corner and demand why she'd abandoned her post behind the bar. When she glanced in the bathroom mirror that morning, however, she discovered the mirror image of a fifty-six-year-old woman who no longer had to answer to the likes of Elliott Plymouth. Although she would never be free of her love for him, she was now free of the prison he'd once built for her. In every sense, her life was now a choice.

Marcy agreed to meet Kurt at the ferry docks at four-thirty that afternoon with only a suitcase and hardly a plan. A few hours before, she had paid her bills, cleaned her kitchen, and eaten some peanuts and raisins, her favorite snack. Her suitcase waited for her at the door, expectant for a life she'd never planned for.

Suddenly, her phone dinged. It was a message from her

bank asking that she call in. Marcy did so immediately, wanting to clear up any problems before she and Kurt skipped town.

"Hi, there. This is Marcy Plymouth."

"Hey there, Marcy." The bank teller was a woman about ten years older than Marcy, who'd worked at the bank longer than Marcy had at the Pink Pony. "I wanted to let you know that we had another request for a transfer of funds. An even bigger one than last time."

Marcy's throat tightened. "How much?"

"He wants to transfer you one million dollars."

Marcy's thoughts blurred. She blinked to the ground, on the brink of passing out.

"This is the fourth time in twenty years that Zane Hamlet has attempted to transfer funds to your account," the bank teller reminded Marcy, as though Marcy wasn't aware of it. "All you have to do is say the word, and you'll be set up for the rest of your life, Marcy."

Marcy knew this wasn't the way normal bank tellers spoke to their clients. The thought of one million dollars was enough to change the tune.

But just as she had the previous three times, Marcy coughed and said, "I have to refuse."

"Think of the rest of your life, Marcy. You'd be able to stop working at the bar. You could move to Florida or France or wherever else you want to," the bank teller continued, pleading with her. Under her breath, she added, "We all know what he did to you. Why don't you just take the money? Set yourself up good?"

"Thank you for the call," Marcy said instead. "But I really am sure." After that, she hung up the phone.

Marcy still had a bit of time before she needed to meet Kurt at the ferry docks. Very quickly, she packed a backpack of things, tugged on her autumn jacket, and fled toward the forest behind the Pontiac Trail Head. The air was fresh and clear, and with each stride, thoughts about the million dollars she'd refused fell off of her like dead skin.

If she allowed herself, Marcy could feel Zane wherever he was in the world. She could feel his regret and his shame for having left her behind. And for that, she pitied him.

Marcy had never wanted Zane's money. She'd only wanted the love that they'd built together. When he'd left, that love had been destroyed. It no longer existed— not in the air nor the water nor the sands nor the trees. It certainly couldn't be found in a one-million-dollar transfer into her account.

Fifteen minutes into her hike, Marcy reached an area of the forest that had once been cleared of trees. Over the years, new trees had pummelled through the soil and stretched their leaves toward the sky. You could still see where the new trees ended and the old trees began, but Marcy knew that very soon, that distinction wouldn't be so clear.

There, Marcy collapsed against an old birch, closed her eyes, and listened to the soft ache of her breath. Between these old trees, Zane had planned to build them a gorgeous summer home. *"We can bring our children there. They will know the island just as well as we do,"* he'd said so long ago.

For years, Marcy had had nightmares about the life she'd planned to have with Zane. In her dreams, she'd been pregnant with his babies, painting nurseries and laughing in his arms. In several, Zane and Elliott had finally gotten along and joined together to teach her son how to throw a baseball. In another, they'd gathered at the fireplace of the beautiful house that Zane had designed, their eyes tired from a full day beneath the island sun.

Marcy fumbled through the things in her backpack before she pulled out the envelope. Within, she'd tucked all the remaining photographs she still had of herself and Zane during the era when they'd been in love. Each presented an all-American couple, their arms wrapped around one another, their muscles shining, and their legs long. In twenty-one-year-old Marcy's eyes, optimism shimmered. That version of Marcy had known something that fifty-six-year-old Marcy no longer did.

Gently, Marcy kissed the top of each photograph and then snapped her father's old lighter against the top right corner. Immediately, a flame nibbled at the edge of each photograph and then ate through the pretty images. Very soon, Marcy had nothing to show of that long-lost life. She slipped her backpack back on her shoulders, set her jaw, and headed back through the woods.

Marcy was three minutes early to meet Kurt at the ferry docks. Kurt was already there, jittery and wearing a big grin.

"I was fifteen minutes early," he confessed, just before Marcy rushed into his arms, closed her eyes, and kissed him with all the love she had.

Kurt and Marcy stood on the top deck of the ferry and watched the mainland come toward them. Once the ferry latched to the dock, they waved goodbye to the ferry captain and the ferry workers and headed to Marcy's car, which Kurt drove out of the garage.

Before the ultimate escape could begin, both knew they had a stop to make.

It was Marcy's third time at the nursing home that week. Each time, she'd noticed slight advancements in Elliott's condition. Once, he'd half-smiled at her. Another time, he'd been more animated upon her arrival, waving his hand.

This time, the doctor reported that by next week, Elliott would begin to relearn how to walk. Marcy wrapped her arms around her father joyously, grateful that she wouldn't have to say goodbye just yet.

"Did you hear that, Dad?" Marcy said as they settled him in front of the television again. "You're going to be feeling a whole lot better in no time."

Elliott's eyes followed Marcy as she traipsed up and down

the little nursing home suite, setting up Thanksgiving decorations and bouquets of fake flowers. Kurt helped, placing a candle on the table and a wreath in the bathroom. They then sat with Elliott for about an hour, chatting with him about what was happening on the island. Marcy talked at length about Elise's wedding to Wayne Tanton, whom Elliott had always liked.

"Remember, you always said he was an upstanding man?" Marcy reminded her father, who couldn't respond. "It was such a tragedy when his wife passed away. But Elise is a wonderful person. Just a breath of fresh air on that island of ours."

Kurt nodded and spoke easily to Elliott, whom he'd known his entire life. "You'd have hated the food, though. Not enough meat."

"That's right!" Marcy laughed. "They had an all-fish wedding meal and two types of salads. You would have complained the entire time."

One half of Elliott's face lifted into a smile, followed briefly by the second half. Elise knew, in some part of herself, that Elliott appreciated the goodwill and the jokes. She prayed that he could feel the extent of her love for him wherever he was in there.

Later, Marcy kissed her father goodbye and said that she would be back next week.

"Not too long," Kurt confirmed as he took Marcy's hand. "But long enough. Your daughter needs a break."

Once in the car, Kurt started the engine and slid his sunglasses up his nose. There in the silence of the vehicle, Marcy closed her eyes and felt the autumn sun tickle her cheeks.

"What do you say, Marcy?" Kurt said with a wry smile. "You think we ought to follow the sun?"

Marcy's laughter sizzled with surprise. "Are you saying what I think you're saying?"

Kurt nodded firmly. "I think it's high time we take that trip to Florida. We've only been talking about it for thirty-five years."

"I guess it's now or never," Marcy agreed, her eyes filling with tears.

Chapter Twenty-One

Brad's decision to take a couple of months off from LA came as a welcome surprise. The breakup, along with Brad's general malaise about his current job, had gotten Brad to talk to Dean and Wayne alone a few nights after the wedding. Both Wayne and Dean had insisted that life was too short to remain in a place of hardship. On top of that, Wayne reminded Brad that they could use another pair of hands around Mackinac as the house on the hill required a number of repairs. Dean offered one of the upstairs rooms at his place, and Wayne bought a few more tools for the months ahead. Even Michael snapped into action, welcoming Brad to the island with a rowdy night out at the Pink Pony.

Penny's flight back to California was set for the same day that Elise and Wayne headed out for their honeymoon. Cindy and Tracey drove them down to Detroit, grateful to grab an extra few hours of conversation. Penny, who was always the over-dramatic actress, cried for a few minutes about her brother's decision to leave California. "It's the end of an era," she said. Elise reminded her that Penny always had a place on

Mackinac, but that she supported her on her journey to become a renowned actress.

At the airport, both Cindy and Tracey hugged Elise and Wayne, demanding at least fifty photos per day via text message. Elise reminded them that they would only be gone for two weeks, saying, "Thanksgiving is right around the corner. You know that Wayne and I would never miss all that food."

Elise managed to walk Penny all the way to her boarding gate, where she tucked a strand of blond hair around her daughter's ear and whispered, "Thank you for making my wedding day one of the best of my life." To this, Penny winked and said, "I hope that Wayne knows that I was the one who made it that special." Elise cackled with tears in her eyes. "You're your grandmother's granddaughter. I hope you know that."

On the flight, Elise and Wayne sat in first class and ordered two glasses of wine, olives, and little slices of cheese and salami. Out the window, a thick blanket of clouds separated them from the wide stretch of the continent below. Their conversation bubbled and popped with excitement, but when Wayne became quiet for a moment, Elise turned his wedding band around and around his finger and whispered, "I love you." Something about being so far above the rest of the world made the sentiment even more true.

The plane landed in Nassau at six that evening, which was only thirty-one minutes before the sunset. Wayne and Elise leaped into a taxi and asked that they be taken to the "best sunset close by." The driver gave them a firm nod and pressed the gas, whipping them through traffic like his life depended on it. Once they reached the westward-facing beach, Wayne dug through his bag and removed two plastic cups and a bottle of French champagne, wagging his eyebrows knowingly.

"How did you sneak that here?" Elise shrieked.

Wayne laughed. "I have my ways." He tugged the cork from the bottle and filled both cups, his skin glowing with the orange and pink light of the Bahamas sun. Elise kicked her feet to the side and wiggled her toes in the sand as the bubbles of the champagne sizzled across her tongue. When Wayne kissed her, the kiss was different than it had been before their marriage; this kiss was from a man who'd made a lifelong promise to love her.

When the sun dipped into the water and flashed its final light across the waves, Elise and Wayne poured themselves another round of drinks and stretched out on a towel, slowly relaxing beneath the warmth of the southern sun. Nassau was one thousand four hundred and ninety-two miles from Mackinac. It was another planet.

"What do you think we'll be like when we're old?" Elise asked, surprising herself with the softness of her voice.

Wayne considered this for a moment, his hand stretched across the naked skin of her stomach. "You'll be a knockout. That's for sure."

Elise shivered with laughter. "Stop it. I'll be a little old lady."

"A hot little old lady," Wayne teased. "You know it's true."

Elise laughed again, burrowing her head against his chest. "Okay. Okay. But what else?"

"All right. I'll play." Wayne raised his eyebrows. "I think we'll be very playful. Always teasing each other the way we do now. But we'll be even better about it by then because we'll have that much more ammunition against one another."

"I see that marriage, to you, is just more ammunition."

"Sure. I already know so many of your quirks, Elise Darby Tanton. But after another forty years of this, I'll know everything. Every. Thing. So, you had better watch yourself."

Elise and Wayne's giggles echoed down the empty beach.

"You'd better watch yourself as well," Elise quipped.

"Oh, I plan to," Wayne said. "I won't let my guard down for

a second. Even when we're ninety years old, I'll watch you like a hawk."

Elise's heart lifted. For a long and beautiful moment, they gazed into one another's eyes, both grateful for the choice of falling in love. They would fight for what they had every single day of their lives. Elise imagined herself slowly stirring up the birthday cake for Wayne's ninetieth, love in each step.

When darkness fell completely over the beach, Wayne called them an Uber, which took them to the resort they'd booked for the first part of their vacation. There, two young men took their suitcases to their suite. The suite was airy, with floor-to-ceiling windows that opened out to the beach beyond. A little kitchenette was stocked with bottles of wine, champagne, beer, fruit, and snacks. A thick stack of fresh towels sat on the bed, a reminder that for the next two weeks, someone else would be taking care of all household tasks. All Elise and Wayne had to do was relax.

They'd decided to have a late seafood dinner at the resort restaurant at nine. Elise hung up her clothes in the closet and hunted through her toiletries bag to redo her makeup. Wayne stretched out on the bed and chatted to Elise happily, never once glancing at his phone. It was as though the rest of the world no longer existed.

Just then, a surprise DING came from Elise's phone.

"Hey! I thought we weren't communicating with the outside world," Wayne teased.

Elise laughed. "I'm sorry. I thought that I turned off the sound." She grabbed her phone from her purse to turn it off, only to find a very peculiar notification on the screen. Her eyes widened.

"What's up?" Wayne asked, leaning against his elbow on the bed.

Elise shivered with laughter. "Marcy Plymouth just sent me a friend request."

Wayne's lips parted with surprise. "Marcy Plymouth has a social media account?"

Elise nodded, clicking through to look at the profile. She then jumped back on the bed to show Wayne, who hung his head over her shoulder and peered down.

"Looks like she just made it," Elise said as they peered at the only photo that Marcy had uploaded so far. In it, Marcy had her arms around Kurt's waist as they stood out on a blissful-looking beach somewhere with the sun shining behind them. The beach didn't look entirely unlike the one that Wayne and Elise had just watched the sunset on.

"She looks completely different," Wayne muttered.

"She looks happy," Elise breathed. "I don't think I've ever seen her so happy."

"That Kurt has been in love with her for years," Wayne affirmed. "Everyone has always known it. But I never thought in a million years that she would open her heart to him."

Elise lifted her shoulder knowingly. In all the days since she and Brad had met Zane Hamlet out in Los Angeles, she'd kept the story of Marcy's abandonment to herself. Perhaps one day, she would tell Wayne what she knew; perhaps she wouldn't. In any case, that story was Marcy's story— and it seemed clear that Marcy was more than ready to forget about it.

Elise was dressed in a dark green dress that fluttered across her thighs and slid her feet into a pair of sleek heels. Her hair danced beautifully down the tops of her arms. Wayne wore a pair of jeans and a suit jacket, his smile confident as he guided her to the resort restaurant. Once there, they shared a platter of Bahamian Boiled Fish which hummed with butter and garlic and cloves, some cracked conch with lime, and a bottle of white wine. Around them, couples from all walks of life celebrated the loyalty they had to one another— their eyes alight with love as they swapped stories from either decades together or only months.

Wayne lifted his glass to toast Elise, but soon stuttered with disbelief. Finally, he mustered, "I don't know what I would have done if you hadn't come into my life."

Elise could feel that sentiment echo across the dining room, through each suite of the Bahamian resort, across the islands, and up through the United States of America. *What would any of us do without the love that sustained us?* Elise thought now, her heart in her throat. Her eyes closed, she breathed, "I wouldn't be who I am today without your love."

They clinked glasses and drank to the promise of their future. Together, they could be better than they'd ever been before.

Coming Next in the Secrets of Mackinac Island

You can now Pre Order Mackinac Heritage

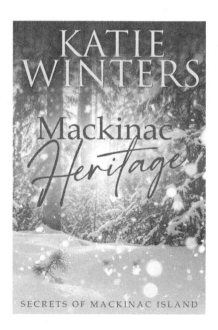

Other Books by Katie

The Vineyard Sunset Series

A Nantucket Sunset Series

Secrets of Mackinac Island Series

Sisters of Edgartown Series

A Katama Bay Series

A Mount Desert Island Series

Connect with Katie Winters

Amazon
BookBub
Facebook
Newsletter

To receive exclusive updates from Katie Winters please sign up
to be on her Newsletter!
CLICK HERE TO SUBSCRIBE

Made in United States
North Haven, CT
09 February 2023

32329976R00095